喚醒你的英文語感！

Get a Feel for English !

喚醒你的英文語感！

Get a Feel for English !

作者◉ 商英教父
Quentin Brand

愈忙愈要學
英文字串
社交篇

BIZ ENGLISH
for
BUSY PEOPLE
Mini Book

附 1 片 MP3 擴展你的人脈版圖

貝塔語言出版
Beta Multimedia Publishing

懂得交際，才能掌握敲定生意的關鍵！

有人說，在高爾夫球場上敲定的生意比在會議室裡還多。的確，雖然想法或提案是在會議室裡討論與評估，但做成決定的場合往往是後來的酒吧或餐廳，因為生意和人有關，也和信任與交情有關。

在全球化的時代裡，以非母語來交際以及跟來自其他文化的人建立商業網絡是一項重要的商業技巧。無論是和重要的舊夥伴維持良好的關係，還是和新夥伴建立互信，這種技巧都不可或缺。有企圖心的生意人可能會想辦法改善寫英文電子郵件或是做英文簡報的技巧，但不要忽略了，改善洽談與交際的技巧也很重要。不過，由於洽談牽涉到跨文化的溝通；交際則牽涉到談論生意以外的話題。所以這也意謂著你要對別人敞開心胸、談論你的看法，並和他們分享一些個人的觀點與人生經驗。

本書分享了一些洽談技巧，並提供適用於各個交際場合的實用用語，以協助各位不再畏懼以英語和外國人交際。希望能幫助各位更輕鬆地找到生意夥伴，並成為一個更懂得交際的人。

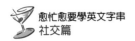

愈忙愈要學英文字串
社交篇

架構與使用說明

架 構

本書架構分為二部分：一為「心法篇」、二為「實踐篇」。

心法篇：說明 Leximodel 字串學習法的效用和注意事項；
也分享一些洽談生意的技巧。

實踐篇：以主題為區分，提供和生意伙伴交際時的必備字
串，並佐以例句和範文幫助讀者學會字串用法。

使用說明

社交字串

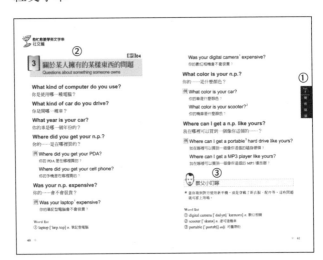

① 依章節主題作為側標，方便查詢。

② 社交字串的主題。

③ 教父小叮嚀：針對字串的用法提供詳細解說，並提醒易犯的錯誤；或是提點與老外交際時的注意事項。

對話範例

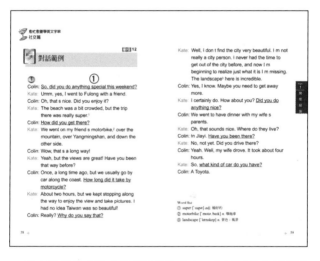

① 畫底線部分為該章節所提供的字串，你可以藉由範例學會字串的用法。

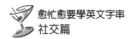
縮寫代碼

sb. = somebody（某人）。

V = verb（動詞）。

Ving = verb ending in -ing（動詞接 -ing）。

p.p. = past participle（過去分詞）。

n.p. = noun phrase（名詞片語），就是 word partnership，不含動詞或主詞。

   例：financial news

      cost reduction

clause = clause（子句），一定包含主詞和動詞。

   例：<u>I need</u> your help.

      What <u>is your estimate</u>?

wh-clause = 以 who、whoever、where、when、what、whether、how 開頭的名詞子句。

   例：I don't know <u>who you are</u>.

      <u>Where you live</u> is not important.

CONTENTS

Part 6 談論電影

Part 7 談論音樂

Section 1

心法篇

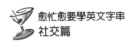

Leximodel 字串學習法

以前的教學法教你學好文法，然後套用句子，用這方法學習有如牛步。現今 Leximodel 幫助了許多人充分開發英文潛能，其基礎概念是從字串（multi-word items; MWI）的層面來看語言，所有的字串可分成三大類：word partnerships、chunks 和 set-phrases，並且可依其可預測的程度區分，可預測度愈高的一端是固定字串，可預測度愈低的一端是流動字串。學習英文由字串著手，投資報酬率遠高於死 K 文法、死背單字。

The Spectrum of Predictability
可預測度

fixed 固定			fluid 流動
	set-phrases	chunks	word partnerships

三類字串當中，word partnerships 的流動性最高。舉例來說，English 這個字後面可以接的字有很多可能性，如：class、book、teacher、email 或 grammar 等，你很難正確預測。由於很難預測、流動性

高，我們稱此類字串爲流動字串（fluid）。

Chunks 字串則含有固定和流動元素。... listen to ... 即爲一個很好的例子：listen 後面總是接 to，這是其固定元素；但 ... listen ... 可以是 ... are listening ...、... listened ...、have not been listening carefully enough ...，這些則是 listen 的流動元素。

Set-phrases 是最固定的字串，通常字串較長，可能包括句子的句首或句尾，甚至兩者兼具，換句話說，有時 set-phrases 會是一個完整的句子。例如社交對談中常可見到的 set-phrases：What do you think of it? 或 Do you know what I mean?。學會 set-phrases 的一大優點，就是在用法上絲毫不須費神操心文法問題，所以本書提供的用語大部分是 set-phrases，你只要原原本本照用即可。

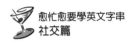
學習 Set-phrases 的注意事項

　　學習和使用 set-phrases 時，需要注意的細節有三大類：

1. 短字（如：a、the、to、in、at、on 和 but）。這些字很難記，但是瞭解了這點，即可以說是跨出一大步了。Set-phrases 極為固定，用錯一個短字，整個 set-phrase 都會改變，等於是寫錯了。

2. 字尾（有些字的字尾是-ed，有些是-ing，有些是-ment，有些是-s，或者沒有-s）。字尾改變了，字的意思也會隨之改變。Set-phrases 極為固定，寫錯其中一字的字尾，整個 set-phrase 都會改變，等於是寫錯了。

3. Set-phrases 的結尾（有的 set-phrase 以 clause 結尾，有的以 n.p. 結尾，有的以 V 結尾，有的以 Ving 結尾）。許多人犯錯，問題即出在這些地方。學習 set-phrases 時，必須將結尾部分記牢。Set-phrases 極為固定，結尾用錯，整個 set-phrase 都會改變，等於是寫錯了。

Leximodel 問與答

你大概心裡覺得 Leximodel 的概念好像不錯，但腹中仍有疑問吧？這樣吧，看看你是否能從下列關於 Leximodel 的常見 Q&A 中獲得解答。

Q：我該如何實際運用 Leximodel 學英文？為什麼 Leximodel 和我以前碰到的英文教學法截然不同？

A：簡而言之，只要熟悉字串的組合和這些組合的固定程度，就能簡化英語學習的過程，同時大幅減少犯錯的機率。以前的教學法教你學好文法，然後套用句子，稍不小心就會錯誤百出，想必你早就有切身的體驗。現在只要用 Leximodel 建立 chunks、set-phrases 和 word partnerships 語庫，接著只需背起來就能將英文運用自如。

Q：這本書如何以 Leximodel 幫助我用英文和客戶建立良好關係？

A：本書提供了各類社交常見字串（chunks、set-phrases

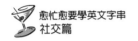

和 word partnerships，以 set-phrases 為最多），只要原原本本照用就可輕鬆和客戶交際，建立良好合作關係。

Q：如果沒有文法規則可循，我怎麼知道自己的 set-phrases 用法正確無誤？

A：很簡單，本書提供了社交所需的各類字串。你只需確定自己運用的 set-phrases 和書中的一模一樣即可。注意在「學習 set-phrases 的注意事項」中提及的所有細節。別擔心你用的 set-phrases 運用或違反了哪些文法規則，只要參照本書的字串準沒錯。

東西方談話比一比

文化差異在擴展人際和交際談話中扮演了重要的角色。這些文化差異不大，所以很多人都沒有注意到，但假如你想更有效地擴展人脈並成為交際高手的話，了解它們就很重要。

我在好幾年前第一次到台灣學中文時，我想要交新朋友，於是在咖啡廳、公車上或酒吧裡跟人聊天。當時我並不曉得亞洲人和西方人在談話風格上的文化差異，所以我當然是用西方人的談話方式。雖然跟我交談的台灣人都很友善，我也的確交到了一些好朋友，但我卻開始對自己的交際能力感到不滿意。我想著，「我到底是怎麼了？」在英國的時候，我是個善於交際的人，而且很容易就能跟別人聊開來。可是到了台灣，就算我朋友的英文好得不得了，為什麼我卻老是覺得交際是件難事？後來有一天，有一個台灣朋友告訴我，我是個話很多的人，而且老愛問一大堆問題。但我之所以會問這麼多問題，是因為我想讓談話延續下去。於是我便開始思考亞洲人和西方人在談話風格上的差異。當我在亞洲各

23

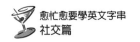
地旅行時,我開始聆聽周遭的人的談話方式,以下是我的心得。

1. 亞洲人比西方人習慣談話中的沈默。西方人對於談話中的沈默會覺得不自在,所以他們會用很多方式來讓談話進行下去。

2. 西方人比較常問問題,這不是因為他們話多,而是因為如果要讓別人開口,問問題是再平常不過的方法。而且在西方人的談話中,談話高手就是指懂得怎麼讓對方開口的人。

3. 西方人喜歡對各式各樣自己不一定很懂的話題表示意見。比方說,西方人覺得自己不必是政治專家,但也可以對政治情勢發表看法。又比方說,他們覺得自己不一定是音樂專家,但也會對自己喜不喜歡哪種音樂以及為什麼發表看法。但另一方面,亞洲人則被教導應該要謙虛,不要對自己不太懂的東西發表意見。

　　當然,這是非常概括的推論,所以各位也許並不認同我在上面所提到的一些看法。但是透過觀察,尤其是聆聽周遭的談話,我發現下列的方式真的很有用。你在

和外國人交談時，可以把這些心得歸納成三個非常有用的原則來記，相信對於促進合作關係會有正面的助益：

1. 讓談話進行下去，盡量避免令人不自在的沈默。

2. 不要害怕問對方問題，尤其是關於看法的問題。

3. 不要害怕表達自己的意見。如果對方表達了他對某件事的看法，你也要表達自己的意見，就算意見相左也無所謂。

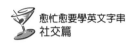
成為談話高手的小撇步 1

1. 選一個你有把握談論的話題；或是讓對方選擇話題，
   然後積極參與談話

   ・假如你對於對方所談的話題一無所知，那就請他解
   釋給你聽，從基本項目開始談起。

   ・不妨針對幾個話題準備相關字彙，並設法把談話引
   導到這些話題上。利用「開啓話頭」單元所教的用
   語來發問，就可以做到這點。

   ・你所選擇的話題應該取決於你對談話對象的熟悉
   度，以及他的文化背景。

   ・安全又有趣的話題包括：運動、興趣、下榻旅館、
   衣服、飲食、渡假計畫、共同的經驗。安全但可能
   乏味的話題包括：天氣、樂透、工作、手邊的案
   子、生涯規畫。

   ・應避免的話題有：政治、性、宗教、健康。

   ・應謹慎的話題有：家庭、雙方都認識的人、時事。

2. 不要害怕表達自己的意見

   ・西方人慣於先表達自己的看法，然後再聽別人的意

見。如果他們表達完自己的看法，你卻沒有表示意見，他們會覺得很奇怪。

· 外國人很樂於發表看法，即使不是針對自己專長的領域，所以當他們問你有什麼看法時，盡量不要說：「我不知道。」因為這樣會使談話無法進行。

· 假如你對於所討論的話題沒有意見，編也要編一個出來！

· 你的意見不一定得和對方一致。但如果你的意見完全對立，也不須表現出強硬的態度，只要適度表達立場即可。

3. 記住外國名人的英文名字

· 要讓社交談話變得比較容易，很重要的一點在於：記住名人的英文名字。不管是歷史人物、新聞中的現代人物、運動員，還是名流。在你的談話中他們都可以派上用場。

· 遺憾的是，你不能指望外國人記住名人的中文名字。

· 盡量記住一些最近讀過的英文書名，即使你讀的是

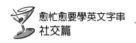

中譯本也一樣。

· 記住你喜歡或最近看過的電影的英文片名，以及片中主要演員的英文名字。

· 練習這些名字的發音，以便能把它們清楚、自信地唸出來。

4. 掌握自己的興趣的相關字彙

· 如果你有某項興趣，確定自己能夠談論它的細節。可以在浴室裡對著鏡子練習解說。你也可以找個同伴或是網路聊天室，練習或是觀察別人如何談論自己的興趣。

· 舉例來說，當對方的嗜好是收集與品嚐法國紅酒，你就可以告訴他，你一直想要了解法國紅酒，可是從來不知道該問誰。接著請他談些相關的基本訊息，並對他所說的話表現出興趣。

· 平時應該針對本身的嗜好或興趣吸取相關知識，這可以幫助你增進字彙，讓你有話可聊。

· 如果你沒有嗜好或興趣，那就去找一個！

成為談話高手的小撇步 2

1. 讓對方「多」說一點

· 大部分的人都喜歡有機會談論自己，或是表達自己的意見；大部分的人也都喜歡有個好的聆聽者，能對自己所說的每件事點頭稱許。

· 假如你能讓對方多說一點，這就表示你可以少說一點！如此一來，你就不必太過擔心自己的說話技巧和語彙不足的問題。

· 假如你能讓對方多說一點，並當個好聽眾，你就會贏得談話高手的美名；如此一來，你的人際關係自然會好！

2. 問有趣的問題

· 如果要鼓勵對方多說一點並當個好聽眾，你就必須問些有趣的問題。各位可以在「開啟話頭」的單元中學到這些用語。

· 西方人喜歡談論自己的興趣和意見，而不喜歡談論自己的家庭生活；但台灣人往往相反。所以在問問

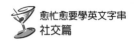

題時，要盡量問對方的興趣，而不要問他的私人生活。

· 盡量避免問無聊的問題。我有一位外國朋友在台灣住了好幾年，她在名片上印了下列資料：

1. 我沒有結婚。

2. 我沒有生小孩。

3. 我會說中文。

這些年來，不斷回答同樣的問題已經使她不勝其擾，於是她就把答案印在名片上，好讓自己不必再回答！

3. 設法了解對方

· 有很多人擔心，不知道該和陌生人或者必須交際的人談些「什麼」。假如你把焦點擺在對方而不是自己身上，不要去管必須和他交談讓你有多煩惱，那你就不會覺得那麼緊張了。

· 設法找出一些雙方共有的興趣或經驗，然後談論這些話題。

· 你可能會發現，對方跟你去過同一個國家渡假，此
時你們就可以針對這個經驗交換意見。

· 你可能會發現，你們對電影的喜惡相同，此時你們
就可以談論電影。

· 你可能會發現，自己的小孩和對方的小孩年齡相
仿。此時你們就可以談談爲人父母的煩惱、壓力及
樂趣。

· 不用擔心該談些「什麼」，只要設法去認識對方就
好。盡量在最短的時間內成爲他的朋友。

4. 假裝很有興趣

· 在社交談話中，重要的不是說了「什麼」，而是友善
的互動所形成的「感覺」。對對方所說的話表示興趣
有助於形成這種良好的感覺。

· 對方在說話時，你要保持笑容、表示興趣並點點
頭，然後說：That's really interesting!「真是有趣
極了！」或 What do you mean?「你的意思是什
麼？」假如你無法全部聽懂，但對方似乎對這個話
題很有興趣，那你也要表現出興致高昂的樣子。

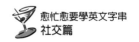

· 相信我，假如對方從頭講到尾，而且覺得你對他說
的話很感興趣，他就「不會注意到」你談自己談得
不多。

5. 假裝聽懂他人所說的話

· 假如你不確定對方在說什麼，那就假裝聽懂，然後
多問一些問題，像是 What do you mean by that?
「你這麼說的意思是什麼？」，直到自己開始聽懂為
止。

· 不要一直想著下列的問題：要是我聽不懂他的話怎
麼辦？要是他的腔調很重，或者我的聽力不好怎麼
辦？

· 讓對方放鬆並樂於談論自己，這樣他可能甚至不會
注意到你大概只聽懂一半他所說的話。

Section 2

實踐篇

🍷 Part 1
開啟話頭

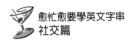
MP3 02

1 一陣子沒見到某人時可以問的問題
Questions you can ask when you haven't seen some-one for a while

What have you been doing since I saw you last?

自從我上次見到你，你都在做些什麼？

Have you been busy?

你最近在忙嗎？

What did you do over the weekend?

你週末做了些什麼？

Did you do anything special this weekend?

你這個週末有沒有做什麼特別的事？

How was your holiday/weekend/trip/ vacation?

你的假日／週末／旅行／假期如何？

How are you?

你好嗎？

Is everything going well?
一切都還好嗎？

How's it going?
最近如何？

How's business?
生意如何？

What happened?
發生了什麼事？

What have you been doing this week?
你這個星期都在做些什麼？

Where have you been?
你跑到哪裡去了？

 教父小叮嚀

⊙ 在英式英語中，「休假」為 holiday；美式英文為 vacation。

⊙ How's it going? 是 How are you? 的非正式說法。

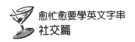

MP3 03

2 關於某人未來計畫的問題
Questions about someone's future plans

What are you doing this weekend?
你這個週末要做些什麼？

Are you doing anything nice this weekend?
你這個週末有要做什麼好玩的事嗎？

Are you doing anything special this weekend?
你這個週末有要做什麼特別的事嗎？

What are you planning on doing for your next vacation?
你下一次休假預計要做些什麼呢？

Are you going out later?
你等一下要出去嗎？

What are you thinking of doing next?
你接下來想做什麼？

Where are you going to go ...?
你……要去哪裡？

例 Where are you going to go over the weekend?
你週末要去哪裡？

Where are you going to go Spring Festival?

你春假要去哪裡？

Any plans for n.p.?

……有任何計畫嗎？

例 Any plans for the weekend?

週末有任何計畫嗎？

Any plans for the holiday?

假日有任何計畫嗎？

Do you always want to work in n.p?

你一直都想要在……工作嗎？

例 Do you always want to work in marketing?

你一直都想要在行銷界工作嗎？

Do you always want to work in finance?

你一直都想要在金融界工作嗎？

Are you going to n.p./V?

你要去……嗎？

例 Are you going to Colin's party tomorrow?

你明天要去柯林的派對嗎？

Are you going to see the new Batman movie?

你要去看那部新的蝙蝠俠電影嗎？

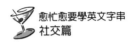
MP3 04

3 關於某人擁有的某樣東西的問題
Questions about something someone owns

What kind of computer do you use?
你是使用哪一種電腦？

What kind of car do you drive?
你是開哪一種車？

What year is your car?
你的車是哪一個年份的？

Where did you get your n.p.?
你的……是在哪裡買的？

例 Where did you get your PDA?
　你的 PDA 是在哪裡買的？

Where did you get your cell phone?
　你的手機是在哪裡買的？

Was your n.p. expensive?
你的……會不會很貴？

例 Was your laptop[1] expensive?
　你的筆記型電腦會不會很貴？

Word list
① laptop [ˈlæp.tɑp] *n.* 筆記型電腦

Was your digital camera[1] expensive?

你的數位相機會不會很貴？

What color is your n.p.?

你的……是什麼顏色？

例 What color is your car?

你的車是什麼顏色？

What color is your scooter?[2]

你的機車是什麼顏色？

Where can I get a n.p. like yours?

我在哪裡可以買到一個像你這個的……？

例 Where can I get a portable[3] hard drive like yours?

我在哪裡可以買到一個像你這個的隨身硬碟？

Where can I get a MP3 player like yours?

我在哪裡可以買到一個像你這個的 MP3 播放器？

教父小叮嚀

● 當你看到對方使用新手機，或是穿戴了新衣服、配件等，這些問題就可派上用場。

Word list

① digital camera [`dɪdʒɪt] `kæmərə] *n.* 數位相機

② scooter [`skutɚ] *n.* 速可達機車

③ portable [`portəbl] *adj.* 可攜帶的

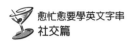
MP3 05

4 關於某人過去經歷或職涯的問題
Questions about someone's past experiences or career

What did you major in?
你主修什麼？

Where did you go to college?
你唸哪裏的大學？

Which university did you go to?
你就讀哪一所大學？

Where did you work before?
你之前在哪裡工作？

Where did you live before coming here?
你搬來這裡之前是住在哪裡？

Have you been to n.p.?

你有去過……嗎？

例 Have you been to Beijing?

你有去過北京嗎？

Have you been to Disneyland?

你有去過迪士尼樂園嗎？

Have you ever p.p.?

你有……過嗎？

例 Have you ever eaten frog's legs?

你有吃過田雞的腿嗎？

Have you ever seen a Chinese opera?

你有看過京劇嗎？

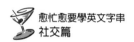

5 關於某人看法的問題

MP3 06

Questions about someone's views

What do you think of the current (...) situation?

你覺得目前的（……）狀況如何？

例 What do you think of the current situation?

你覺得目前的狀況如何？

What do you think of the current economic situation?

你覺得目前的經濟狀況如何？

What do you think of the long-term (...) prospects?[1]

你覺得長期的（……）展望如何？

例 What do you think of the long-term prospects?

你覺得長期的展望如何？

What do you think of the long-term investment prospects?

你覺得長期的投資展望如何？

Word list

①prospect [ˈprɑspɛkt] *n.* 展望；前途

What do you think of n.p.?

你覺得⋯⋯如何？

例 What do you think of our new boss?

你覺得我們的新上司如何？

What do you think of the latest marketing plan?

你覺得最新的行銷計畫如何？

What are your views on n.p.?

你對於⋯⋯有何看法？

例 What are your views on the new government regulations?

你對於這項新的政府規範有何看法？

What are your views on the violence in the Middle East?

你對於中東的戰亂有何看法？

Did you read that report on ... in ...?

你讀了⋯⋯關於⋯⋯的報導嗎？

例 Did you read that report on Taiwan in *The Economist*?

你讀了《經濟學人》裡那篇關於台灣的報導嗎？

Did you read that report on China's financial markets in the *Asia Business Review*?

你讀了《亞洲商業評論》裡那篇關於中國金融市場的報導嗎?

Have you seen this?

你有看過這個嗎?

教父小叮嚀

● 西方人喜歡回答和本身看法有關的問題,不喜歡回答與家人或家務有關的問題;亞洲人則相反。在和不同國家的人交際時,要記得這點。

● 政治是個敏感的話題,在談論時要小心。

● 在 Did you read that report on ... in ...? 這個字串中,on 後面是接「主題」,in 後面則是接看到報導的地方。

6 關於工作的問題
Questions about work

How is your company coping[1] with the economic situation?
你的公司如何應付這個經濟狀況？

How do you do this in your company?
你在公司裏怎麼處理這件事？

How does your company deal with n.p.?
你們公司如何處理……？

例 How does your company deal with government regulations?
你們公司如何應付政府規範？

How does your company deal with late payment?
你們公司如何處理延遲的款項？

How did n.p. go?
……進行得怎麼樣？

例 How did your presentation go?
你的簡報進行得怎麼樣？

How did the meeting with your client go?
你和客戶的會議進行得怎麼樣？

Word list
① cope [kop] *v.* 妥善處理；對抗

Did n.p. go well?

……進行得順利嗎？

例 Did the interview go well?

面試進行得順利嗎？

Did the training session[1] go well?

訓練課程進行得順利嗎？

Do you get along with your coworkers?

你和你的同事相處融洽嗎？

What are you working on at the moment?

你目前在做什麼？

教父小叮嚀

● 工作雖然不是有趣的主題，但卻是用來打破沈默的好辦法。它是個
  安全的主題。此外，有些人熱愛工作，或是工作之外沒什麼特別的
  興趣，所以還是得學會如何談論工作。

Word list

① session ['sɛʃən] *n.* 講習會；集會

7 關於某人目前生活型態的問題
Questions about someone's current lifestyle

How long have you been here?
你來這裡多久了？

Where do you live?
你住哪裡？

Do you live far from the office?
你住得離公司遠嗎？

How do you get to work?
你怎麼來上班？

How long does it take you to get ...?
你到……要多久？

例 How long does it take you to get home?
你到家要多久？

How long does it take you to get to the office?
你到公司要多久？

Do you have your family with you?
你有帶家人一起來嗎？

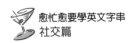
How many children do you have?
你有幾個小孩？

Do your children like it here?
你的小孩喜歡這裡嗎？

Where are you sending them to school?
你送他們去哪裡上學？

Do you/they miss home?
你／他們想家嗎？

What does your wife/husband do?
你的太太／先生是做什麼的？

Does he/she like it here?
他／她喜歡這裡嗎？

What are you reading at the moment?
你現在在讀些什麼書？

What are you doing at the moment?
你現在在做些什麼事？

教父小叮嚀

◉ 如果你知道對方的家人也一起住在當地，其中一些句子就可派上用場。

8 第一次遇到某人時可以問的問題

Questions you can ask someone you are meeting for the first time

How do you do?
你好嗎？

Where did you grow up?
你是在哪裡長大的？

Where are you from?
你從哪裡來？

What do you do?
你是做什麼的？

Where do you work?
你在哪裡工作？

Who do you work for?
你替誰工作？

What department do you work in?
你在哪個部門工作？

What does your company do?
你的公司是做什麼的？

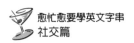
How long have you worked there?
你在那裡工作多久了？

What's your job title?
你的職稱是什麼？

How big is your company?
你的公司有多大？

Where is it based?[1]
它在哪裡？

How do you like it here?
你覺得這裏如何？

Are you married?
你結婚了嗎？

How long have you been married?
你結婚多久了？

Do you have any children?
你有小孩嗎？

Can you speak Chinese?
你會說中文嗎？

Word list
① base [bes] *v.* 以……爲根據地

Where did you learn n.p.?

你在哪裡學……的？

例 Where did you learn Chinese?

你在哪裏學中文的？

Where did you learn how to cook?

你在哪裏學烹飪的？

教父小叮嚀

- 這些問題和對已熟識的人提出的問題不一樣。比較中立，是在對別人的生活和工作建立基本認識。
- 在問 Are you married? 和 Do you have any children? 這些問題時要小心，因為可能會冒犯到想結婚但還沒結婚、或是想要小孩但還沒有小孩的人。對西方人來說，離婚不是禁忌話題，如果對方主動提及不用覺得尷尬，但可不要再追問下去。

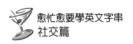
MP3 10

9 關於某人興趣和嗜好的問題
Questions about someone's interests and hobbies

What's your handicap?[1]
你的差點是多少？

How long have you been playing?
你從事（某活動）多久了？

Where do you play?
你在哪裡從事（某活動）？

Are you a member?
你是會員嗎？

Are you a new member?
你是新會員嗎？

How long have you been a member?
你成為會員多久了？

Do you play any sports?
你有從事任何運動嗎？

Do you play any other sports?
你會從事任何其他的運動嗎？

Word list
① handicap ［ˋhændɪˌkæp］ *n.*【運動】差點

What do you do in your free time?
你空閒時都做些什麼？

Have you seen n.p.?
你有看過……嗎？

例 Have you seen the new Batman movie?
你有看過新的蝙蝠俠電影嗎？

Have you seen *The Godfather*?
你有看過《教父》嗎？

What kind of n.p. do you like?
你喜歡哪一種……？

例 What kind of movies do you like?
你喜歡哪一種電影？

What kind of outdoor activities do you like?
你喜歡哪一種戶外活動？

Have you ever played n.p.?
你有玩過……嗎？

例 Have you ever played mahjong?
你有玩過麻將嗎？

Have you ever played volleyball?
你有玩過排球嗎？

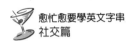
Have you ever been Ving?

你有……過嗎？

例 Have you ever been bowling?

你有打過保齡球嗎？

Have you ever been white water rafting[1] in Hualian?

你有在花蓮玩過急流泛舟嗎？

教父小叮嚀

● What's your handicap? 是高爾夫球用語。打高爾夫球的人喜歡討論差點，以顯示他們的技術水準。差點愈低，代表球打得愈好。初學者的差點可能在 30 以上，技術好的人差點可能不到 5。假如你遇到老虎伍茲，千萬不要問他的差點，因為職業選手是不用差點的。

● 千萬不要用 What's your hobby? 來詢問對方的嗜好，因為聽起來很幼稚。

● Have you ever played ...? 後面通常接的是「球類活動」；Have you ever been ...? 後面通常接的是「體能活動」。

Word list

① raft [ræft] v. 乘筏航行

10 鼓勵某人打開話匣子的問題
Questions to encourage someone to talk more

Why do you say that?
你爲什麼那麼說？

What do you mean by that?
你那麼說是什麼意思？

Why is that?
爲什麼是那樣？

Why?
爲什麼？

What does that mean?
那是什麼意思？

What makes you say that?
你爲什麼會那麼說？

 教父小叮嚀

- 這些問題能鼓勵別人多說些話，自己也就能少開口，是減輕自己壓力的好方法。
- 這些字串中，that 指的是對方提過的某一點或是話題。

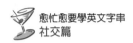

 對話範例

Colin: <u>So, did you do anything special this weekend?</u>

Kate: Umm, yes, I went to Fulong with a friend.

Colin: Oh, that's nice. Did you enjoy it?

Kate: The beach was a bit crowded, but the trip there was really super.[1]

Colin: <u>How did you get there?</u>

Kate: We went on my friend's motorbike,[2] over the mountain, over Yangmingshan, and down the other side.

Colin: Wow, that's a long way!

Kate: Yeah, but the views are great! Have you been that way before?

Colin: Once, a long time ago, but we usually go by car along the coast. <u>How long did it take by motorcycle?</u>

Kate: About two hours, but we kept stopping along the way to enjoy the view and take pictures. I had no idea Taiwan was so beautiful!

Colin: Really? <u>Why do you say that?</u>

Kate: Well, I don't find the city very beautiful. I'm not really a city person. I never had the time to get out of the city before, and now I'm beginning to realize just what it is I'm missing. The landscape[3] here is incredible.

Colin: Yes, I know. Maybe you need to get away more.

Kate: I certainly do. How about you? <u>Did you do anything nice?</u>

Colin: We went to have dinner with my wife's parents.

Kate: Oh, that sounds nice. Where do they live?

Colin: In Jiayi. <u>Have you been there?</u>

Kate: No, not yet. Did you drive there?

Colin: Yeah. Well, my wife drove. It took about four hours.

Kate: So, <u>what kind of car do you have?</u>

Colin: A Toyota.

Word list

① super [ˋsupɚ] *adj.* 極好的
② motorbike [ˋmotɚ͵baɪk] *n.* 摩拖車
③ landscape [ˋlænskep] *n.* 景色；風景

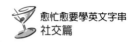

柯林：所以，妳在這個週末有沒有做什麼特別的事？

凱特：呃，有，我和朋友去了福隆。

柯林：喔，不錯。玩得開心嗎？

凱特：開心，海灘上有點擠，不過一路上都很棒。

柯林：妳們是怎麼去的？

凱特：我們騎我朋友的摩托車爬過陽明山，然後下到另一邊。

柯林：哇，好長一段路啊！

凱特：是啊，可是風景不錯！你以前有走過哪條路嗎？

柯林：有，很久以前，可是我們通常是沿著海岸開車去。騎車花了多少時間？

凱特：大概兩個小時，不過我們沿路都有停下來欣賞風景與拍照。我不知道台灣竟然這麼美！

柯林：是嗎？妳為什麼那麼說？

凱特：哦，我並不覺得這個城市很美，而且我根本不是個喜歡城裡生活的人。以前我從來沒有時間出市區，現在我才開始明白我錯過了些什麼。這裡的景觀美極了。

柯林：是啊，我知道。也許妳需要更常出來走走。

凱特：我當然會。你呢？你有沒有做什麼開心的事？

柯林：我們去找我岳父母吃飯。

凱特：噢，聽起來不錯。他們住在哪兒？

柯林：嘉義。妳去過那裡嗎？

凱特：沒有，還沒去過。你們是開車去的嗎？

柯林：是，我太太開的車，大概開了四個小時。

凱特：那你們是開哪種車去？

柯林：Toyota ……

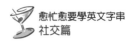
②

Kate: <u>Where did you get your mobile?</u>[1] It's really cute.

Brad: Oh, this? I got it in Singapore. Here, do you want to take a look?

Kate: Thanks. Gee, it's really light!

Brad: Yes, it is, isn't it? A bit too light, really. What make[2] have you got?

Kate: I've got an old Ericsson. Here. Take a look.

Brad: Wow, that's really old.

Kate: Yes, I like collecting antiques.[3] *(laughter)*

Brad: Why don't you get a new one?

Kate: I don't know. I like this one, and I don't have any need for all the bells and whistles[4] you get on the new ones.

Brad: Really, <u>what makes you say that?</u>

Kate: Well, I just need to make and receive calls, and it's quite reliable. I find that the more fancy stuff they put into these things, the more likely they are to break down or malfunction, you know? I mean, this camera function, for instance. How often do you use it?

Brad: Sometimes, but I guess not very often. It's more for fun. Umm, when I'm on a trip, for example, I can take pictures and send them to my nieces and nephews. Or, for work, I can send a picture of a sample back to the office and get it priced right away. That's handy.[5]

Kate: Well, that is useful. *(Pause)* So, you're an uncle. How many nieces and nephews do you have?

Brad: Three. Two nephews and a niece. The oldest is ...

(the conversation continues)

Word list

① mobile ['mobɪl] *n.* 行動電話

② make [mek] *n.* 型式

③ antique [æn'tik] *n.* 古物；骨董

④ all the bells and whistles 各式各樣的東西

⑤ handy ['hændɪ] *adj.* 方便的；合用的

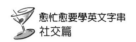

凱　特：你的手機是在哪裡買的？好可愛。

布萊德：哦，這支嗎？我在新加坡買的。妳要看看嗎？

凱　特：謝謝。哇，好輕！

布萊德：是啊，它的確很輕。說真的，它太輕了一點。妳用的是哪一款？

凱　特：我用的是老式的 Ericsson。你拿去看看。

布萊德：哇，真老舊啊。

凱　特：是啊，我喜歡收集骨董。（笑）

布萊德：妳為什麼不換一支新的？

凱　特：我也不知道。我就是喜歡這支，而且我根本不需要像你的新手機一樣有那些各式各樣的功能。

布萊德：是哦，妳為什麼這麼說？

凱　特：哦，我只需要接打電話而已，這方面它很可靠。你知道嗎，我發現具備愈多花俏功能的手機，就愈容易壞掉或故障。我的意思是，就拿這種照相的功能來說，你有多常用到？

布萊德：有時候，不過我想不會很常用，而是以好玩為主。例如有時候在旅行時，我可以拍照，然後寄給我的姪女和姪兒看。在工作方面，我也可以把樣品的照片寄回辦公室，以便立刻估價。非常方便。

凱　特：嗯，那很有用。（停頓一下）所以你是個叔叔了，你
　　　　有幾個姪女如姪兒呢？

布萊德：三個，兩個姪兒一個姪女。最大的是⋯⋯

（談話繼續）

🍷 Part 2
回應話頭

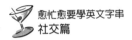

MP3 13

1 表達意見
Expressing your opinion

In my opinion, + clause.

依我看來，……。

例 In my opinion, it's not one of her best movies.

依我看來，這不是她最棒的電影之一。

In my opinion, modern music is pretty awful.

依我看來，現代音樂挺難聽的。

I personally think + clause.

我個人覺得……。

例 I personally think part one was better than part two.

我個人覺得第一部比第二部要好。

I personally think it's one of his best albums.

我個人覺得這是他最棒的專輯之一。

If you ask me, + clause.

如果你問我，……。

例 If you ask me, French movies are overrated.[1]

如果你問我，法國電影是名過其實。

Word list
① overrate [ˌovəˈret] v. 高估

If you ask me, her music is not as good as it used to be.

如果你問我，她的音樂沒有以前那麼好了。

I think + clause.

我認為……。

例 I think Chinese art is great.

我認為中國藝術很棒。

I think it's difficult to understand.

我認為這很難理解。

I reckon[1] + clause.

我覺得……。

例 I reckon it's impossible to get good bread here.

我覺得要在這裡買到好麵包是不可能的事。

I reckon this is one of the best books I've ever read.

我覺得這是我所讀過最好的書之一。

My view is that + clause.

我的看法是……。

例 My view is that the situation will improve before long.

我的看法是，這個狀況不久後就會改善。

Word list

① reckon [ˈrɛkən] v. 認為

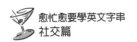

My view is that now is a very good time to invest.

我的看法是，現在是一個投資的大好時機。

I'm convinced that + clause.

我確信……。

例 I'm convinced that they're trying to improve the economy.

我確信他們正試著要改善經濟。

I'm convinced that things are going to get worse before they get better.

我確信事態會在好轉前惡化。

I'd say that + clause.

我會說……。

例 I'd say that Vietnam is a good place to invest right now.

我會說越南現在是個投資的好地方。

I'd say that German is more difficult to learn than English.

我會說德文比英文難學。

I suspect that + clause.

我懷疑……。

例 I suspect that they don't really know what they are doing.

我懷疑他們並不真的知道自己在做什麼。

I suspect that Colin and Kate are having an affair.

我懷疑柯林和凱特有一腿。

Many people think that + clause, but actually + clause.

許多人認為……，但實際上……。

例 Many people think that French wine is the best, but actually I prefer wine from South America.

許多人認為法國酒是最好的，但實際上我比較喜歡南美的酒。

Many people think that it's difficult to learn Chinese, but actually it's easier than you think it is.

許多人認為中文很難學，但實際上它比你想像的要容易。

In my experience, + clause.

在我的經驗裡，……。

例 In my experience, these things always die down[1] eventually.

在我的經驗裡，這些事情最後總會平息下來。

Word list
① die down 平息；變弱；逐漸消失

In my experience, it's always more difficult than it seems.

在我的經驗裡，事情總是比看起來要困難。

Clause, don't you think?

……，你不覺得嗎？

例 He's pretty good in that movie, don't you think?

他在那部電影裡表現得很好，你不覺得嗎？

She's so beautiful, don't you think?

她好美，你不覺得嗎？

 教父小叮嚀

◉ 練習發音時，記得重音是在 I 或 my。如：In *my* opinion, ... 或 *I* think that ....，而不是 In my *opinion*, ... 或 I *think* that ....。

2 表示同意
Expressing agreement

Oh yes.
噢，沒錯。

例 A: I think she's fantastic.
B: Oh yes.

A：我認為她棒透了。
B：噢，沒錯。

A: It's a great book.
B: Oh yes.

A：這是本好書。
B：噢，沒錯。

Absolutely!
一點都沒錯！

例 A: It's her best movie!
B: Absolutely!

A：這是她最好的電影！
B：一點都沒錯！

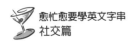

A: It's a great musical!

B: Absolutely!

A：這是部很讚的音樂劇！

B：一點都沒錯！

Definitely!

絕對是！

例 A: It's the best place I've ever visited.

B: Definitely!

A：這是我去過最棒的地方。

B：絕對是！

A: He's the best CEO we've ever had!

B: Definitely!

A：他是我們有過最好的總裁！

B：絕對是！

Indeed!

的確是！

例 A: I thought it was great.

B: Indeed!

A：我認為它很棒。

B：的確是！

A: I thought it was rubbish.[1]

B: Indeed!

A：我認為它遜透了。

B：的確是！

That's for sure.

那是毫無疑問的。

例 A: You know, it's easy to say that, but difficult to do.

B: That's for sure.

A：你知道，說的容易，做起來卻很難。

B：那是毫無疑問的。

A: Well, there are some good American cars, you know.

B: That's for sure.

A：嗯，你知道的，有一些美國車是不錯的。

B：那是毫無疑問的。

Of course!

當然！

例 A: It was so interesting.

B: Of course!

A：真是太有趣了。

B：當然！

Word list

① rubbish ［ˋrʌbɪʃ］ *n.* 垃圾；廢物

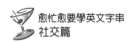

A: Fascinating[1] presentation, don't you think?

B: Of course!

A：很有趣的簡報，你不覺得嗎？

B：當然！

I agree.
我同意。

例 A: I think her voice gets better and better.

B: I agree.

A：我認為她的聲音愈來愈好了。

B：我同意。

A: We should invest now.

B: I agree.

A：我們應該現在就投資。

B：我同意。

I agree completely.
我完全同意。

例 A: I've never thought she was very good.

B: I agree completely.

A：我從來沒想過她居然這麼厲害。

B：我完全同意。

Word list

① fascinating [ˋfæsn̩.etɪŋ] *adj.* 有趣的；迷人的

A: I think it's their best album yet.

B: I agree completely.

A：我認為這是他們目前為止最好的專輯。

B：我完全同意。

I agree with you.

我同意你的看法。

例 A: It's so relaxing and peaceful there.

B: I agree with you.

A：那裡好輕鬆、好平靜。

B：我同意你的看法。

A: Yoyo Ma is such a great artist.

B: I agree with you.

A：馬友友實在是個很棒的藝術家。

B：我同意你的看法。

Exactly!

沒錯！

例 A: It's too crazy and I can't understand the point.

B: Exactly!

A：這實在太瘋狂了，我沒辦法了解箇中含意。

B：沒錯！

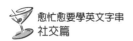

A: It's just what we needed!

B: Exactly!

A：這正是我們所需要的！

B：沒錯！

Well, that's exactly what I always say.

嗯，那正是我一直掛在嘴邊的。

例 A: It's important to relax on vacation.

B: Well, that's exactly what I always say.

A：在度假時放鬆是很重要的。

B：嗯，那正是我一直掛在嘴邊的。

A: High risk yields[1] high returns.

B: Well, that's exactly what I always say.

A：高風險帶來高獲利。

B：嗯，那正是我一直掛在嘴邊的。

Yes, I know exactly what you mean.

沒錯，我完全知道你是什麼意思。

例 A: This wine has a funny aftertaste.[2]

B: Yes, I know exactly what you mean.

A：這個酒有種怪怪的後味。

B：沒錯，我完全知道你是什麼意思。

Word list

① yield [jild] *v.* 帶來（收益等）

② aftertaste [ˋæftɚ͵test] *n.* 餘味；後味

A: There's something wrong with this soup.

B: Yes, I know exactly what you mean.

A：這個湯有點不對勁。

B：沒錯，我完全知道你是什麼意思。

That's right.

沒錯。

例 A: He's so stupid.

B: That's right.

A：他真是有夠笨。

B：沒錯。

A: Tony Blair is sexy.

B: That's right.

A：湯尼・布萊爾很性感。

B：沒錯。

You're not wrong about that!

你說的沒錯！

例 A: It's terrible!

B: You're not wrong about that!

A：太可怕了！。

B：你說的沒錯！

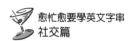
A: Phew! It's hot today!

B: You're not wrong about that!

A：呼！今天好熱！

B：你說的沒錯！

3 表示不同意
Expressing disagreement

Yes, but + clause.
沒錯，但是……。

例 A: I don't like French wine.

B: Yes, but don't you think that there are a few good French wines?

A：我不喜歡法國酒。

B：沒錯，但是你難道不認為有一些法國酒是不錯的嗎？

A: He's a terrible actor.

B: Yes, but sometimes he is quite funny.

A：他是個很糟的演員。

B：沒錯，但是有時候他還滿好笑的。

But the problem is that + clause.
但問題是……。

例 A: I think he's a great writer.

B: But the problem is that it's often difficult to understand his books.

A：我認為他是個很棒的作家。

B：但問題是他的書太難理解了。

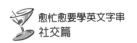
A: I like Joni Mitchell.

B: But the problem is that she's not very well
known here.

A：我喜歡瓊妮‧米契爾。

B：但問題是她在這裡的知名度不高。

Possibly, but + clause.

也許吧，可是……。

例 A: I think it's a pretty safe investment.

B: Possibly, but there are always risks.

A：我認為這是筆相當安全的投資。

B：也許吧，可是風險總是存在。

A: I think Hillary Clinton would be a great
president.

B: Possibly, but I'm not sure that many people
would agree with you.

A：我認為希拉蕊‧柯林頓會是個好總統。

B：也許吧，可是我不確定會有很多人同意你的看法。

What bothers me is that + clause.

我擔心的是……。

例 A: I think you should wait for the exchange rate to improve first.

B: What bothers me is that the exchange rate could get worse.

A：我認為你應該先等匯率好轉。

B：我擔心的是，匯率可能會轉壞。

A: Investing in property[1] in China is a pretty safe bet.

B: What bothers me is that they could introduce a heavy capital gains[2] tax.

A：投資中國地產是個相當保險的賭注。

B：我擔心的是，他們可能會實行高資本增值稅。

What bothers me is the n.p.

我擔心的是……。

例 A: The global economy can only get better.

B: What bothers me is the possibility of a slump[3] in the price of oil.

A：全球經濟只會變得更好。

B：我擔心的是油價暴跌的可能性。

Word list

① property [ˈprɑpətɪ] *n.* 地產；財產

② gain [gen] *n.* 盈餘；利潤

③ slump [slʌmp] *n.* 暴跌

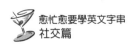
A: The economy is pretty solid.[1]

B: What bothers me is the risk of another political crisis.

A：經濟還挺穩固的。

B：我擔心的是另一場政治危機的風險。

Yes, but don't forget that + clause.

沒錯，但是別忘了……。

例 A: It's just going to get worse and worse.

B: Yes, but don't forget that it might also get better first.

A：情況只會愈來愈糟。

B：沒錯，但是別忘了它也可能先轉好。

A: They say they won't increase taxes.

B: Yes, but don't forget that they always say that.

A：他們說他們不會增稅。

B：沒錯，但是別忘了他們總是那麼說。

Yes, but don't forget ....

沒錯，但是別忘了……。

Word list

① solid [ˋsɑlɪd] *adj.* 穩固的

例 A: Their movies are terrible.

B: Yes, but don't forget the first one they did. That was excellent, don't you think?

A：他們的電影很爛。

B：沒錯，但是別忘了他們拍的第一部。那一部棒極了，你不覺得嗎？

A: Their movies are excellent.

B: Yes, but don't forget the last movie they made was terrible.

A：他們的電影很棒。

B：沒錯，但是別忘了他們拍的上一部電影很爛。

That's probably true, but + clause.

也許是如此，但是……。

例 A: It wasn't as good as the previous one they did.

B: That's probably true, but I still say it's the best one I've ever seen.

A：這沒有他們拍的上一部好。

B：也許是如此，但我還是覺得這是我看過最棒的一部。

A: She's a bit limited as an artist.

B: That's probably true, but I like her anyway.

A：她身為一個藝術家的才藝有限。

B：也許是如此，但是我還是喜歡她。

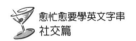
But on the other hand, + clause.

但話說回來，……。

例 A: I think you should invest immediately.

B: But on the other hand, it might be too soon.

A：我認為你應該馬上投資。

B：但是話說回來，現在可能太快了。

A: They make a great couple.

B: But on the other hand, don't you think she's too old for him?

A：他們是很適合的一對。

B：但是話說回來，你不覺得她配他有點太老了嗎？

Yes, but look at it this way: + clause.

是啊，但從這個角度來看，……。

例 A: I think the risk is way too high.

B: Yes, but look at it this way: the high risk might yield a high return.

A：我認為風險實在太高了。

B：是啊，可是換個角度來看，高風險可能會帶來高獲利。

A: It tastes good, but it's a bit overpriced.[1]

B: Yes, but look at it this way: the price you pay is worth the taste.

A：嚐起來味道不錯，但是價格有點過高。

B：是啊，可是換個角度來看，一分錢一分貨啊。

Very true, but + clause.

的確是，但是……。

例 A: It's one of the smallest but most profitable[2] companies in the market.

B: Very true, but I heard them say they were going to merge.[3]

A：它是市場中最小但是獲利最高的公司之一。

B：的確是，但是我聽他們說他們要合併了。

Part
2
回
應
話
頭

A: This Argentinean[4] wine is excellent.

B: Very true, but I still prefer French wine anyway.

A：這種阿根廷酒非常好。

B：的確是，但是我還是比較喜歡法國酒。

Word list

① overprice [ˌovəˈpraɪs] *v.* 對……索價過高；將……定價過高

② profitable [ˈprɑfɪtəbl] *adj.* 有獲利的；有利的

③ merge [mɝdʒ] *v.* 合併

④ Argentinean [ˌɑrdʒənˈtɪnɪən] *adj.* 阿根廷的

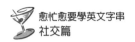
Hmm. I'll have to think about that.

嗯……，這我得想一想。

例 A: It's total rubbish, this music.

B: Hmm. I'll have to think about that.

A：這音樂爛透了。

B：嗯……，這我得想一想。

A: George W. Bush was the greatest president since Kennedy.

B: Hmm. I'll have to think about that.

A：喬治‧布希是自甘迺迪以來最棒的總統。

B：嗯……，這我得想一想。

Oh, rubbish!

噢，鬼扯！

例 A: Angelina Jolie is the greatest actress who ever lived.

B: Oh, rubbish!

A：安潔莉娜‧裘莉是有史以來最棒的女演員。

B：噢，鬼扯！

A: Brad Pitt is a genius.

B: Oh, rubbish!

A：布萊德‧彼特是個天才。

B：噢，鬼扯！

Come on, you can't be serious!

拜託，你不會是認真的吧！

例 A: *The Da Vinci Code* is a great work of
literature.

B: Come on, you can't be serious!

A：《達文西密碼》是一部文學鉅著。

B：拜託，你不會是認真的吧！

A: Jazz doesn't have any meaning. It's just noise.

B: Come on, you can't be serious!

A：爵士沒有任何的意義，只是噪音罷了。

B：拜託，你不可能是認真的吧！

I don't see it quite like that.

我的看法不是這樣。

例 A: I know it was my fault but that doesn't mean I
should be fired.

B: I don't see it quite like that.

A：我知道這是我的錯，但那不表示我應該被開除。

B：我的看法不是這樣。

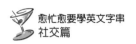
A: Their economy is just going to get worse and worse.

B: I don't see it quite like that.

A：他們的經濟只會愈來愈糟。

B：我的看法不是這樣。

 教父小叮嚀

- 在表達不同意時，如果希望語氣婉轉一些，就不要直接說 No.。可以改說： Yes, but .... 或 Yes, but don't forget that ....。

- Oh, rubbish! 和 Come on, you can't be serious! 都是用來表達強烈的不同意。和不熟的人應對時，應該避免使用這二個字串。

4 表示興趣
Showing interest

OK.

是喔。

例 A: I went to this party a few days ago

B: OK.

A：我幾天前去參加了這個派對。

B：是喔。

A: I saw Mary there.

B: OK.

A：我在那裡見到了瑪麗。

B：是喔。

And then?

然後呢？

例 A: So I walked in and there was no one there!

B: And then?

A：所以我走了進去，裡面一個人都沒有！

B：然後呢？

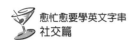
A: Mike was drunk.

B: And then?

A：麥克喝醉了。

B：然後呢？

Really?

真的嗎？

例 A: I saw her the other day in the supermarket.

B: Really?

A：我前幾天在超市看到她。

B：真的嗎？

A: She made a pass at[1] me.

B: Really?

A：她挑逗我。

B：真的嗎？

Oh my God, you're kidding me!

噢，天啊，你是在開玩笑吧！

例 A: I've won the lottery!

B: Oh my God, you're kidding me!

A：我中了樂透！

B：噢，天啊，你是在開玩笑吧！

Word list

① make a pass at 向……調情；挑逗……

A: I've been promoted. I'm your new boss.

B: Oh my God, you're kidding me!

A：我升職了。我是你的新上司。

B：噢，天啊，你是在開玩笑吧！

No kidding!

真的假的！

例 A: I got promoted!

B: No kidding!

A：我升職了！

B：真的假的！

A: John got fired!

B: No kidding!

A：約翰被開除了。

B：真的假的！

Oh, that's good.

喔，那很好。

例 A: I'm having a day off tomorrow.

B: Oh, that's good.

A：我明天休一天的假。

B：喔，那很好。

A: My client just placed a huge order.

B: Oh, that's good.

A：我的客戶剛剛下了一張大訂單。

B：喔，那很好。

How wonderful!

真好！

例 A: My wife is pregnant!

B: How wonderful!

A：我太太懷孕了！

B：真好！

A: We're going to Florida for Chinese New Year.

B: How wonderful!

A：我們要去佛羅里達過農曆新年。

B：真好！

How terrible for you!

你真慘！

例 A: I just got fired!

B: How terrible for you!

A：我剛被開除了！

B：你真慘！

A: My mother-in-law is coming to live with us.

B: How terrible for you!

A：我的岳母要來和我們一起住。

B：你真慘！

How awful!

太慘了！

例 A: I crashed my car this morning!

B: How awful!

A：我今天早上把我的車撞壞了！

B：太慘了！

A: I had my wallet stolen on the train this morning.

B: How awful!

A：我的皮夾今天早上在火車上被偷了。

B：太慘了！

Wow!

哇！

例 A: I'm going to Maui for my vacation.

B: Wow!

A：我要去茂宜島度假。

B：哇！

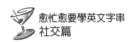

A: Do you like my new car?
B: Wow!

A：你喜歡我的新車嗎？

B：哇！

Yuck![1]

噁！

例 A: I found a cockroach in my hamburger at lunch!
B: Yuck!

A：我吃午飯時在我的漢堡裡發現一隻蟑螂！

B：噁！

A: The waiter was sweating and the sweat was
dripping into the soup!
B: Yuck!

A：服務生在流汗，汗都滴到湯裏了。

B：噁！

Go on.

繼續說。

例 A: So then I told Mike to go away and leave me
alone.
B: Go on.

A：所以我就叫麥克走開，別煩我。

B：繼續說。

Word list

① yuck [jʌk] *interj.* 表示厭惡、拒絕等聲音

A: And then he wanted me to kiss him.

B: Go on.

A：然後他要我親他。

B：繼續說。

No!

不會吧！

例 A: They're getting married again!

B: No!

A：他們又打算結婚了！

B：不會吧！

A: The CEO just resigned.

B: No!

A：總裁剛剛請辭了。

B：不會吧！

Uh-huh.

呃哼。

例 A: And then I told her, I said she was wrong.

B: Uh-huh.

A：然後我告訴她，我說她錯了。

B：呃哼。

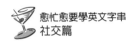
A: And then we went to this amazing Turkish restaurant for dinner.

B: Uh-huh.

A：然後我們去這家很棒的土耳其餐廳吃晚飯。

B：呃哼。

Mmm-hum.

嗯哼。

例 A: It's so hot today

B: Mmm-hum.

A：今天好熱！

B：嗯哼。

A: You want to know what happened to me yesterday?

B: Mmm-hum.

A：你想要知道我昨天發生了什麼事嗎？

B：嗯哼。

 教父小叮嚀

- Oh my God, you're kidding me! 和 No kidding! 這二個字串是用來表示驚訝；How terrible for you. 和 How awful! 用來表示反感；Oh, that's good. 和 How wonderful. 用來表示好感；Yuck! 則用來表示厭惡或噁心。

- 聽 MP3 來練習 Uh-huh. 和 Mmm-hum. 的語調，語調不同可是會傳達出不同的意思喔。

對話範例

Part 2
回
應
話
頭

(at a golf course)

Sandra: Good game?

Colin:　Not bad. Bit too hot for me today.

Sandra: Yes, I know. Kind of hard to concentrate, isn't it?

Colin:　<u>Absolutely</u>. Who were you playing with?

Sandra: Oh, just on my own. I just joined, so I don't really have any partners.

Colin:　<u>Really</u>? Well, in that case, we should play together some time. <u>What's your handicap</u>?

Sandra: Sixteen. Yours?

Colin:　<u>No kidding!</u> I'm sixteen, too. We should definitely play together some time. My name's Colin.

Sandra: Sandra. Nice to meet you.

Colin:　Likewise. So, do you like the course?

Sandra: Yeah, it's great. However, <u>I personally think</u> the fairways[1] between the greens[2] are a bit

Word list

① fairway [ˋfɛr,we] *n.* 美好區；平坦球路

② green [grin] *n.* 果嶺

◆ 99

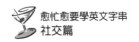

too long, especially for such a hot climate. Don't they have carts?[1]

Colin: Well, they used to, but they got rid of them because of environmental concerns.

Sandra: <u>Oh, that's good.</u> I guess the caddies[2] were pleased.

Colin: Actually, <u>in my opinion</u>, the carts were better because you didn't have to tip them.

Sandra: <u>Yes, but look at it this way:</u> getting rid of the carts probably gives more work to local people, and that is a good thing, right?

Colin: Probably, but I still miss them! <u>What bothers me is that</u> the heat makes the caddies' life quite hard. One member's caddy fainted last week!

Sandra: <u>How awful!</u> Poor guy.

Colin: Yeah. Luckily it was on the eighteenth hole, quite near the clubhouse, so the member didn't have to carry him too far.

Sandra: <u>Oh, my God, you're kidding me!</u> The golfer carried him back?

Colin: Yup. A nice young lady named Kate, I believe ...

Word list

① cart [kɑrt] *n.* 小型手推車
② caddy [ˋkædɪ] *n.* 球僮；桿弟

100

中譯

（在高爾夫球場上）

珊德拉：比賽還好嗎？

柯　林：還不錯。我覺得今天太熱了一點。

珊德拉：是啊，我知道。有點難以定下心來，對吧？

柯　林：沒錯。你跟誰一起打？

珊德拉：喔，我自己打。因為我才剛加入，所以我連個球伴都
　　　　沒有。

柯　林：真的嗎？噢，要是這樣的話，我們應該找個時間一起
　　　　打。你的差點是多少？

珊德拉：十六。你呢？

柯　林：不蓋你！我也是十六。我們一定要找個時間一起打。
　　　　我叫做柯林。

珊德拉：我叫珊德拉，很高興認識你。

柯　林：我也是。對了，你喜歡這個球場嗎？

珊德拉：喜歡，還不錯。不過，我個人覺得果嶺間的球道太長
　　　　了一點，尤其天氣又這麼熱。他們沒有球車嗎？

柯　林：哦，以前有，可是後來基於環保的理由就不用了。

珊德拉：喔，那很好。我猜桿弟會很開心。

柯　林：其實我覺得有球車比較好，因為你不必給小費。

珊德拉：是啊，可是換個角度來看，不用球車或許可以增加本
　　　　地人的就業機會，這也是好事一樁，對吧？

柯　林：也許吧，可是我還是很懷念球車！我擔心的是，酷暑
　　　　會使桿弟的日子變得很難過。上星期就有一位會員的

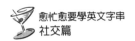

桿弟昏倒了！

珊德拉：太慘了，真可憐。

柯　林：的確。所幸那是在第十八洞，距離會館很近，所以球員不用背很遠。

珊德拉：噢，天啊，你是在開玩笑吧！打高爾夫球的人背桿弟回去？

柯　林：是啊，我想是一位善良年輕、叫凱特的女生。

Kate: Have you seen this?

Brad: What?

Kate: They killed another hostage.[1]

Brad: Oh, <u>how awful.</u> What a terrible thing to do.

Kate: <u>I agree completely.</u> I just don't understand what's wrong with them. Don't they have any humanity?

Brad: Well, maybe they've got a reason. I mean, <u>I suspect that</u> they think the same about us.

Kate: <u>Yes, but</u> that doesn't make it right, does it, just because they think so?

Brad: I guess not. <u>My view is that</u> we should give in to their demands, to keep innocent people for being killed.

Kate: <u>Come on, you can't be serious!</u> We should never give in to terrorists[2] demands! Otherwise, where would we be?

Brad: Well, <u>that's probably true, but I don't think</u> we should be so dogmatic[3] about it. A colleague of mine was kidnapped once, so perhaps I have a different view of things.

Word list

① hostage [ˈhɑstɪdʒ] *n.* 人質

② terrorist [ˈtɛrərɪst] *n.* 恐怖份子

③ dogmatic [dɔɡˈmætɪk] *adj.* 武斷的；獨斷的

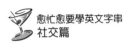

Kate: <u>Really?</u> What happened?

Brad: Well, it was in the Balkans[1] during the war. He was only held for three days, and then they simply released him. It was a case of mistaken identity, and they just let him go when they found out he was no use to them. It was lucky they didn't kill him.

Kate: <u>That's for sure</u>.

Word list
① Balkans [ˋbɔlkənz] *n.* 巴爾幹半島

凱　特：你看了這則報導嗎？

布萊德：什麼？

凱　特：他們又殺了一個人質。

布萊德：噢，太可怕了。這種事真令人髮指。

凱　特：我完全同意。我真是搞不懂他們有什麼毛病。他們連一點人性都沒有嗎？

布萊德：哦，也許他們有他們的道理。我猜他們的想法就跟我們一樣。

凱　特：是，不過這並不表示他們是對的。他們只因為想這麼做，就可以這麼做嗎？

布萊德：當然不是。我的意思是，我們應該接受他們的要求，這樣無辜的人就不會被殺了。

凱　特：拜託，你不是說真的吧？我們絕對不能接受恐怖份子的要求，否則我們要怎麼自處？

布萊德：嗯，這麼說也許沒錯，不過我覺得我們不應該固執己見。我有一位同事被綁架過，所以我對於事情的看法可能不太一樣。

凱　特：真的嗎？那是怎麼回事？

布萊德：哦，那時候巴爾幹半島在打仗。他只被挾持了三天，然後就被釋放了。他們認錯了人，所以等他們發現他沒什麼用處時，他們就把他給放了。所幸他們沒有殺了他。

凱　特：噢，一點也沒錯。

Part 3
延續談話

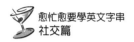

MP3 18

1 起頭
Starting

A funny thing happened to me ....

我……發生一件好玩的事。

例 A funny thing happened to me the other day.

我幾天前發生一件好玩的事。

A funny thing happened to me when I was on vacation.

我去度假時發生一件好玩的事。

Do you remember sb.?

你記得……嗎？

例 Do you remember that guy I told you about last week?

你記得我上週跟你說過的那個人嗎？

Do you remember Mary, that woman who used to work here?

你記得瑪麗嗎？以前在這裡工作的那個女人？

Have you heard the one about n.p.?

你有聽過關於……的那一個嗎？

例 Have you heard the one about the elephant and the mosquito?

你有聽過關於大象和蚊子的那一個嗎？

Have you heard the one about the chicken who crossed the road?

你有聽過關於雞過馬路的那一個嗎？

Have you heard (about) what happened to sb.?

你有沒有聽說……發生了什麼事？

例 Have you heard what happened to Mike?

你有沒有聽說麥克發生了什麼事？

Have you heard about what happened to the boss last night?

你有沒有聽說老闆昨晚發生了什麼事？

I had a funny experience ....

我……有一段有趣的經歷。

例 I had a funny experience when I was in college.

我在大學時有一段有趣的經歷。

I had a funny experience the other day on the bus.

我幾天前在公車上有一段有趣的經歷。

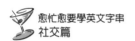
I had a great time ....

我……玩得很開心。

例 I had a great time on vacation.

我度假玩得很開心。

I had a great time at the party last night.

我昨晚在派對上玩得很開心。

I had a terrible ....

我……很慘。

例 I had a terrible weekend.

我週末過得很慘。

I had a terrible time getting home last night.

我昨晚回家的路上很慘。

I heard this really funny joke the other day.

我前幾天聽到這個很好笑的笑話。

I've got a good joke.

我有一個很棒的笑話。

It's about this ....

它是關於一個……

例 It's about this guy who works for a bank and finds
some money missing.

它是關於一個在銀行工作的人，他發現有些錢不見了。

It's about this woman who lives alone in the forest and meets a wolf one day.

它是關於一個在森林裡獨居的女人，有一天她遇到一匹狼。

Have you seen n.p.?

你有看過……嗎？

例 Have you seen Angelina's new baby?

你有看過安潔莉娜的新寶寶嗎？

Have you seen the new Spider-Man movie?

你有看過那部新的蜘蛛人電影嗎？

Have you read n.p.?

你有看過……嗎？

例 Have you read that book I lent you yet?

你看了我借你的那本書沒？

Have you read *The Economist* this week?

你有看過這星期的《經濟學人》嗎？

教父小叮嚀

- Have you heard the one about ...? 中的 the one 指的是 the joke。這個字串是用來介紹笑話。
- It's about this .... 是用來談論電影或書本的內容。

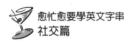

MP3 19

2 鋪陳
Structuring

Well, apparently, ...
嗯，顯然……。

First of all, ...
首先，……。

Then, ...
然後，……。

So then, ...
接著……。

What's more, ...
更有甚者，……。

After that, ...
之後，……。

Finally, ...
最後，……。

In the end, ...
到頭來，……。

例 Well, apparently, he was walking along the road and he saw the guy in front of him drop his wallet. First of all, he didn't know what to do. Then, he decided to at least pick up the wallet and see what was in it. So then, he picked it up and opened it. Inside was a CIA identity card! What's more, the man was licensed[1] to kill! After that, he decided to give the wallet back to the agent[2] immediately. Finally, he managed to catch up with the guy and give him his wallet back. In the end, the guy gave him $100 as a reward for giving him back his wallet!

嗯，顯然他正沿著馬路走，他看到前面那個人掉了他的皮夾。首先，他不知道該怎麼辦。然後，他決定至少要撿起皮夾，看看裡面有什麼。所以他接著把它撿了起來，把它打開。裡面是一張中情局的識別證！更有甚者，那男的可以合法殺人！之後，他決定立刻把皮夾還給那個探員。最後，他設法趕上那個人，並把他的皮夾還給他。到頭來，那個人給了他一百元，當作他歸還皮夾的獎勵！

Word list
① license [ˈlaɪsn̩s] *v.* 特許；認可
② agent [ˈedʒənt] *n.* 特務；間諜

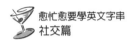
<u>Well, apparently</u>, she locked herself out of her apartment. <u>First of all</u>, she tried to get in through the bathroom window, but it was too small and she nearly got stuck half in and half out. <u>So then</u>, she decided to try another way, and she went up on to the roof and tried to get in that way, but the skylight[1] was locked. <u>Then</u>, it began to rain hard. <u>What's more</u>, the temperature was falling fast and she got worried about freezing to death on the roof. <u>After that</u>, she decided to give up and spend the night in her car. <u>Finally</u>, she got downstairs again to find that she had locked herself out of the car as well! <u>In the end</u>, she had to spend the night in a hotel.

嗯，顯然她把自己反鎖在公寓外頭。首先，她試著要從浴室窗戶進去，但是它太小，她幾乎被卡在那裡進退不得。接著她決定要試試另一個方法，於是她跑到屋頂上，試著要從那裡進去，但是天窗鎖住了。然後，外面開始下起大雨來。更有甚者，溫度開始驟降，她擔心自己會凍死在屋頂上。之後，她決定放棄，打算在她的車裡過夜。最後，她又下了樓梯，卻發現她也把自己反鎖在車外了！到頭來，她不得不在旅館裡度過一晚。

Word list
① skylight [ˈskaɪˌlaɪt] *n.* 天窗

3 重回先前的談話
Returning to a point

So, ...
所以，……。

例 So, that was when he decided to give the wallet back to the guy.

所以，就是在那時他決定要把皮夾還給那個人。

So, after that, she decided to spend the night in the car.

所以，在那之後她決定要在車子裡過夜。

Well, ...
嗯，……。

例 Well, he found a CIA identity card inside.

嗯，他在裡面找到一張中情局的識別證。

Well, the bathroom window was just too small for her to get through.

嗯，浴室的窗戶實在太小，她沒辦法鑽過去。

Part
3
延
續
談
話

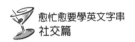

So as I was saying, ...

所以就像我剛才的，……。

例 So as I was saying, he looked through the guy's wallet.

所以就像我剛才說的，他檢查一遍那個人的皮夾。

So as I was saying, it was getting colder and colder up there on the roof.

所以就像我剛才說的，屋頂上面變得愈來愈冷。

Where was I? Oh yes, ...

我說到哪兒了？喔，對了，……。

例 Where was I? Oh yes, he looked through the wallet and guess what he found?

我說到哪兒了？喔，對了，他檢查了一遍那個皮夾，猜猜他找到什麼？

Where was I? Oh yes, the car was also locked!

我說到哪兒了？喔，對了，車子也鎖上了！

Yes, ...

對，……。

例 Yes, it was a shock to him as well.

對，這對他來說也是一大震撼。

Yes, she was getting really cold.

對，她開始覺得非常冷。

Well, anyway, ...

嗯，反正，⋯⋯。

例 Well, anyway, he decided to give the wallet back.

嗯，反正，他決定要歸還那個皮夾。

Well, anyway, she decided to go find a hotel.

嗯，反正，她決定要去找一家旅館。

教父小叮嚀

● 注意這些字串在上個單元的段落範例中如何運用，你會更了解如何
重回先前的談話。

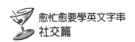
MP3 21

4 回應
Responding

Wow!

哇！

例 A: Well, inside was a CIA identity card.

B: Wow! You mean he was a CIA agent?

A：嗯，裡面是一張中情局的識別證。

B：哇！你是說他是個中情局探員？

A: Then guess what. The car was also locked!

B: Wow! So she had nowhere to spend the night?

A：然後你猜怎麼著。車子也鎖上了！

B：哇！所以她沒有地方可以過夜？

Yes. / Yeah.

是喔。

例 A: He saw the guy drop his wallet.

B: Yes.

A：他看到那個人掉了他的皮夾。

B：是喔。

A: She couldn't get in through the bathroom window.

B: Yeah.

A：她沒辦法從浴室的窗戶進去。

B：是喔。

Mmm.

嗯。

例 A: He was walking along the road.

B: Mmm.

A：他正沿著馬路走著。

B：嗯。

A: It began to get really cold.

B: Mmm.

A：天氣開始變得非常冷。

B：嗯。

Really?

真的嗎？

例 A: He gave him back the wallet.

B: Really?

A：他把皮夾還給他。

B：真的嗎？

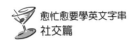

A: She went to a hotel.

B: Really?

A：她去了一家旅館。

B：真的嗎？

OK.

喔。

例 A: He was walking along the road.

B: OK.

A：他正沿著馬路走著。

B：喔。

A: She came home from work very late.

B: OK.

A：她很晚才下班回家。

B：喔。

Right.

沒錯。

例 A: You know, you don't want to mess around[1] with a CIA agent!

B: Right.

A：你知道的，你不會想要和一名中情局探員有牽扯！

B：沒錯。

Word list

① mess around with 惡搞……；和……有牽扯

A: You know, you don't want to sleep outside
   when it's cold and raining!

B: Right.

A：你知道的，天氣又冷又下雨時，你可不會想睡在外面！

B：沒錯。

Oh, no!

噢，不會吧！

例 A: He found a CIA identity card inside the wallet.

B: Oh, no!

A：他在皮夾裡找到一張中情局的識別證。

B：噢，不會吧！

A: And the car was locked too!

B: Oh, no!

A：而且車子也鎖上了！

B：噢，不會吧！

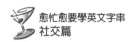
MP3 22

5 鼓勵並示意說話者繼續
Encouraging and signaling a speaker to continue

So what happened next?

所以接下來怎麼了？

例 A: He found a CIA identity card in the wallet!

B: So what happened next?

　A：他在皮夾裡找到一張中情局的識別證！

　B：所以接下來怎麼了？

A: The skylight was locked!

B: So what happened next?

　A：天窗鎖住了！

　B：所以接下來怎麼了？

So what happened?

所以結果呢？

例 A: He found fifteen hundred dollars ($1,500) in the wallet.

B: So what happened?

　A：他在皮夾裡發現了一千五百元。

　B：所以結果呢？

A: The window was too small for her to fit through.

B: So what happened?

A：窗戶太小，她鑽不過去。

B：所以結果呢？

What happened?
結果呢？

例 A: He ran up to the guy and handed him the
　　　wallet.

B: What happened?

A：他追上那個人，把皮夾遞給他。

B：結果呢？

A: The skylight on the roof was locked!

B: What happened?

A：屋頂上的天窗是鎖住的！

B：結果呢？

So then what happened?
所以後來怎麼了？

例 A: He saw the guy drop his wallet.

B: So then what happened?

A：他看到那個人掉了他的皮夾。

B：所以後來怎麼了？

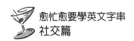

A: She couldn't get in through the window.

B: So then what happened?

A：她沒辦法從窗戶進去。

B：所以後來怎麼了？

And then?

然後呢？

例 A: He saw the guy drop his wallet.

B: And then?

A：他看到那個人掉了他的皮夾。

B：然後呢？

A: She couldn't get in through the bathroom
window.

B: And then?

A：她沒辦法從浴室窗戶進去。

B：然後呢？

You're kidding!

你在開玩笑吧！

例 A: The guy was licensed to kill!

B: You're kidding!

A：那個人可以合法殺人！

B：你在開玩笑吧！

A: The car was locked too!

B: You're kidding!

A：車子也鎖上了！

B：你在開玩笑吧！

You're joking!

你在說笑吧！

例 A: The guy was a professional assassin![1]

B: You're joking!

A：那個人是個職業殺手！

B：你在說笑吧！

A: She climbed up onto the roof!

B: You're joking!

A：她爬到了屋頂上！

B：你在說笑吧！

My God!

我的天！

例 A: The guy dropped his wallet!

B: My God!

A：那個人掉了他的皮夾。

B：我的天！

Word list

① assassin [əˋsæsɪn] *n.* 暗殺者；刺客

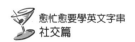
A: The car was also locked!

B: My God!

A：車子也鎖上了！

B：我的天！

What do you mean?

你的意思是什麼？

例 A: He was licensed to kill!

B: What do you mean?

A：他可以合法殺人！

B：你的意思是什麼？

A: She was beginning to freeze.

B: What do you mean?

A：她開始要凍僵了。

B：你的意思是什麼？

Are you serious?

你是認真的嗎？

例 A: The guy who dropped the wallet was a CIA assassin.

B: Are you serious?

A：那個掉了皮夾的人是中情局殺手。

B：你是認真的嗎？

A: She thought she would sleep in the car.

B: Are you serious?

A：她想她要去睡在車子裡。

B：你是認真的嗎？

Yeah, go on.

是喔，繼續說。

例 A: So he opened the wallet to see what was inside.

B: Yeah, go on.

A：所以他打開皮夾看看裡面有什麼。

B：是喔，繼續說。

A: She decided to just sleep in the car.

B: Yeah, go on.

A：她決定去睡車子裡就好。

B：是喔，繼續說。

So what did sb. do?

那……怎麼辦？

例 A: So what did you do?

B: I gave the wallet back.

A：那你怎麼辦？

B：我把皮夾還回去。

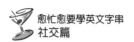
A: So what did they do?

B: They just stayed in a hotel for the night.

A：那他們怎麼辦？

B：他們就在旅館裡過了一夜。

6 評論
Commenting

Sb. sure was (un)lucky.

……真是走運／倒霉。

例 A: So he didn't have to pay excess[1] baggage[2] on his luggage after all!

B: He sure was lucky.

A：所以他終歸是不用付行李的超重運費！

B：他真是走運。

A: So she had to pay a late fee, and a service charge.

B: She sure was unlucky.

A：所以她得付一筆遲繳費和服務費。

B：她真是倒霉。

Sb. was really (un)lucky.

……實在很幸運／倒霉。

Word list

① excess [ɪkˋsɛs] *adj.* 超過的；額外的

② baggage [ˋbægɪdʒ] *n.* 隨身行李

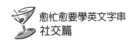
例 A: So he had to pay excess baggage on his
luggage as well!

B: He was really unlucky.

A：所以他還得付行李的超重運費！

B：他實在很倒霉。

A: So she didn't have to pay a late fee, and a
service charge after all!

B: She was really lucky.

A：所以她終歸是不用支付一筆遲繳費和服務費！

B：她實在很幸運。

That's terrible.

太可怕了。

例 A: So they both died in the accident!

B: That's terrible.

A：所以他們兩人都在意外中喪生了！

B：太可怕了。

A: So they lost all their life savings!

B: That's terrible.

A：所以他們失去了一輩子的所有積蓄！

B：太可怕了。

That's amazing.

真是太神奇了。

例 A: It was a magnitude[1] 7.4 earthquake, but no one was injured.

B: That's amazing.

A：那是一場強度 7.4 的地震，但是沒有人受傷。

B：真是太神奇了。

A: So it turned out that he was her brother and she didn't know!

B: That's amazing.

A：所以結果他居然是她的哥哥，而她都不知道！

B：真是太神奇了。

That's incredible.

真是太不可思議了。

例 A: He got a $200,000 year-end bonus by mistake!

B: That's incredible.

A：他誤領了二十萬的年終獎金！

B：真是太不可思議了。

Word list

① magnitude [ˈmæɡnəˌtjud] *n.* 震級

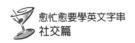
A: She won the lottery, but then she lost the winning ticket!

B: That's incredible.

A：她中了樂透，但是她弄丟了得獎獎券！

B：真是太不可思議了。

That's embarrassing when that happens.

那種事發生時真糗。

例 A: He wanted to introduce them, but he couldn't remember their names!

B: That's embarrassing when that happens.

A：他想要介紹他們，但是卻想不起他們的名字！

B：那種事發生時真糗。

A: She spilled her wine all over the boss's wife!

B: That's embarrassing when that happens.

A：她把酒灑得老闆的妻子滿身都是！

B：那種事發生時真糗。

That's weird.

真詭異。

例 A: The same tree was hit by three different cars on three different Valentine's Days.

B: That's weird.

A：同一棵樹在三個不同的情人節分別被三輛不同的車撞上。

B：真詭異。

A: It was the only tree in the desert for three hundred miles, but they still ran into it!

B: That's weird.

A：這是沙漠三百英哩內唯一的一棵樹，但是他們還是撞上了它！

B：真詭異。

That's gross!

真噁！

例 A: There was a fly in the chow mein!

B: That's gross!

A：炒麵裡有隻蒼蠅！

B：真噁！

A: There was a cockroach sitting on the table waving its feelers[1] at me!

B: That's gross!

A：有隻蟑螂停在桌上對我揮動牠的觸鬚！

B：真噁！

Word list

① feeler [ˋfilə] *n.* 觸鬚

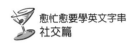
That's a tricky¹ situation.

這種情況不太好處理。

例 A: So he asked me if I wanted to change jobs right in front of my boss!

B: That's a tricky situation.

A：所以他當著我上司的面，問我要不要換工作！

B：這種情況不太好處理。

A: So it turned out that her best friend had been sleeping with her husband!

B: That's a tricky situation.

A：所以結果是她最要好的朋友居然一直在和她的老公上床！

B：這種情況不太好處理。

Word list
① tricky [`trɪkɪ] *adj.* 棘手的；難以處理的

對話範例

Kate: Do you remember Mike from the head office?
Brad: Yes.
Kate: <u>Have you heard</u> what happened to him?
Brad: No, what?
Kate: He had his car stolen. Actually, he was kidnapped while he was in the car.
Brad: What do you mean?
Kate: <u>Well, apparently</u>, he was just getting into his car—he'd parked it in one of those underground multi-story things—he was just getting in and suddenly three guys with guns opened the back doors of the car and got in.
Brad: Crap!¹ Where did this happen?
Kate: In Taichung, I think.
Brad: Oh, right, I hear they have a lot of this kind of problem down there.
Kate: <u>Really</u>? <u>Well, anyway</u>, they pointed their guns at him and said, you know, keep calm and

Word list
① crap [kræp] *interj.* 【表示驚訝】哎呀；唷！

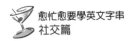
drive. We don't want to hurt you. We just want your car.

Brad: <u>So what happened</u>?

Kate: <u>Well</u>, he drove out, and when he got to the booth[1] to pay the attendant, he pretended to have an epileptic[2] fit—you know, to scare the thieves away. The attendant was no help at all. Even though the guys were holding guns in plain view, he did nothing.

Brad: <u>That's terrible</u>.

Kate: Yes, makes you think, doesn't it?

Brad: <u>So what happened next</u>?

Kate: <u>Well</u>, he kept on pretending to have a fit, so the carjackers[3] freaked out and just ran away.

Brad: <u>Well, he sure was lucky</u>.

Kate: I'll say.

Word list
① booth [buθ] *n.* 攤子;小房間
② epileptic [ˌɛpəˋlɛptɪk] *adj.* 癲癇的
③ carjacker [ˋkɑrˌdʒækə] *n.* 劫持犯

中譯

凱　特：你記得總公司的 Mike 嗎？

布萊德：記得。

凱　特：你有沒有聽說他出了什麼事？

布萊德：沒有。怎麼了？

凱　特：他的車被偷了。他等於是被綁架了，因為他當時在車裡。

布萊德：你的意思是？

凱　特：哦，他顯然是才剛上車，因為他把車停在那些多層式地下停車場的其中一層。他一上車，就有三個持槍的歹徒突然打開後車門跳進去。

布萊德：哎喲。這件事在哪裡發生的？

凱　特：我想是在台中。

布萊德：喔，對，我聽說當地有很多這類的問題。

凱　特：真的嗎？反正他們就拿槍指著他說，靜靜把車開出去就對了。我們不想傷害你，我們只是要你的車而已。

布萊德：所以結果呢？

凱　特：哦，他把車開出去，等開到票亭要繳錢給收費員時，便假裝羊癲瘋發作，你知道，以便把歹徒嚇跑。但收費員根本置之不理，眼睜睜看著那些人拿著槍，他卻袖手旁觀。

布萊德：太可怕了。

凱　特：是啊，你連想都不敢想。

布萊德：所以接下來呢？

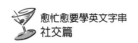
　凱　特：哦，他一直假裝發病，於是他們便嚇得逃走了。
　布萊德：喔，他真是走運。
　凱　特：我也這麼覺得。

2

Brad: <u>I had a terrible journey</u> back from Bangkok last week.

Sandra: <u>Really</u>? Why? <u>What happened</u>?

Brad: <u>Well, first of all</u>, the taxi that was taking me from the client's office to the airport broke down on the freeway.

Sandra: <u>Oh, no</u>.

Brad: <u>Yeah</u>, and the driver didn't speak any English or Chinese and he didn't have a phone on him. Can you believe it? And his radio didn't work. So there was no way he could get in touch with the office to get them to send another taxi.

Sandra: So what did you do?

Brad: <u>Well</u>, I actually hitchhiked.[1]

Sandra: You what? You didn't.

Brad: Yep. I stood on the side of the freeway and stuck out my thumb, and a passing truck stopped and took me to the airport.

Sandra: <u>Wow</u>, good for you.

Word list

① hitchhike [ˈhɪtʃ.haɪk] v. 搭便車

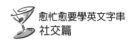

Brad: <u>Right</u>, except the guy drove really slowly and I missed my flight.

Sandra: <u>Oh, no</u>!

Brad: <u>Yeah</u>, so I had to wait three hours for the next one. I didn't get home until four in the morning, and when I got home I realized I'd left my house keys in my hotel in Bangkok.

Sandra: *(laughter)* You really have bad luck, don't you?

Brad: Seems like it.

布萊德：我上週從曼谷回來的時候，過程很驚險。

珊德拉：真的嗎？為什麼？發生什麼事了？

布萊德：哦，首先，計程車在載我從客戶的辦公室到機場的高速公路上拋錨了。

珊德拉：噢，不會吧。

布萊德：是啊，而且司機中英文都不會說，身上又沒電話，你能相信嗎？而且他的無線電又故障了。所以他沒辦法跟總部聯絡，以便派另一輛計程車過來。

珊德拉：那你怎麼辦？

布萊德：哦，我只好搭便車了。

珊德拉：真的嗎？不會吧。

布萊德：是啊，我站在路邊伸出拇指，結果有一輛經過的卡車停下來載我去機場。

珊德拉：哇，真不錯。

布萊德：是啊，只不過他開得很慢，讓我錯過了飛機。

珊德拉：噢，不會吧！

布萊德：是啊，所以我必須等三個小時才有下一班飛機。我一直到清晨四點才到家，而且到家時才發現，我把家裡的鑰匙留在曼谷的飯店裡了。

珊德拉：（笑）你真的很衰耶，對吧？

布萊德：看起來是如此。

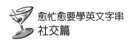

Mike: Do you want to hear a funny joke?

Sandra: <u>OK</u>. Are you sure it's funny, though?

Mike: <u>Well</u>, you'll see.

Sandra: <u>OK</u>.

Mike: <u>OK</u>, an Englishman, a Scotsman, and an Irishman were going on a trip across the desert, and they could only take one thing with them.

Sandra: I see.

Mike: So they met up at the start of the journey and showed each other their equipment.

Sandra: *(Laughter)* Oh, that's funny!

Mike: Hang on, I haven't finished yet.

Sandra: Oh, sorry.

Mike: <u>Well, as I was saying</u>, they showed each other what they had decided to bring. The Englishman had brought some water. "If we get thirsty, we'll have something to drink," he said. The Scotsman brought a map. "If we get lost, we'll be able to find our way." The Irishman had brought a car door.

Sandra: A car door? You mean just one car door?

Mike: Yep. A car door. "Why the door?" the others

asked him. "Well," he said, "If it gets hot, we can open the window." *(Silence)* Do you get it?

Sandra: Am I supposed to laugh?

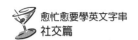

麥　可：你想聽個好笑的笑話嗎？

珊德拉：好啊，可是你確定它好笑嗎？

麥　可：你不妨聽聽看。

珊德拉：好。

麥　可：好，有一個英格蘭人、一個蘇格蘭人和一個愛爾蘭人
　　　　要橫越沙漠，而且每個人只能帶一樣東西。

珊德拉：我懂。

麥　可：於是他們在行程的起點見面時，便把自己的裝備拿給
　　　　其他人看。

珊德拉：（笑）喔，真好玩！

麥　可：等等，我還沒說完。

珊德拉：喔，抱歉。

麥　可：嗯，我說到他們把自己決定要帶的東西拿給其他人
　　　　看。英格蘭人帶了一些水，他說：「假如我們口渴
　　　　了，我們就有東西可以喝。」蘇格蘭人帶了一張地
　　　　圖。「假如我們迷路了，我們就可以靠它來找路。」
　　　　愛爾蘭人則帶了一扇車門。

珊德拉：車門？你是說一扇車門？

麥　可：沒錯，就是車門。另外兩個人問他說：「為什麼要帶
　　　　車門？」他說：「哦，假如天氣熱的話，我們就可以
　　　　把車窗打開。」（沈默）你聽懂了嗎？

珊德拉：我應該要笑嗎？

4

Colin: Have you seen the movie *Catwoman*?

Kate: No, not yet. Is it good?

Colin: <u>Yes</u>, it's quite amusing, actually. Good plot, and Sharon Stone's in it.

Kate: Oh, she's good. She must be starting to show her age.

Colin: <u>Yeah</u>, but she still looks amazing.

Kate: So what's the movie about?

Colin: <u>Well</u>, <u>it's about this</u> woman who gets murdered because she discovers some company secrets for the cosmetics company she works for. But then she gets reincarnated[1] as a cat.

Kate: Huh?

Colin: I know. Stay with me. She then decides to get her revenge by revealing the company secret and killing her boss. <u>First</u>, though, she has to discover her true cat nature. At the end she has a big fight with Sharon Stone's character, who is the real danger behind the company. She is the one who murdered the boss, who was also her husband, and then tries to frame[2]

Part
3
延
續
談
話

Word list
① reincarnate [ˌriin`karnet] *v.* 使……化身為……
② frame [frem] *v.* 陷害；誣陷

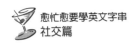
Catwoman for the murder, so everyone thinks
Catwoman is evil.

Kate: I see. Catwoman married the boss?

Colin: No. Sharon Stone's character was married to
the boss, who treated her badly, so she kills
him. <u>So where was I</u>? <u>OK, so then</u>, at the
same time, Catwoman falls in love with a cop
who is investigating the murder of the boss.
<u>Finally</u>, she ditches[1] the cop to follow her
feline[2] nature.

Kate: Wait a minute. I'm lost. The cop killed the
boss?

Colin: No. Sharon Stone did.

Kate: And Sharon Stone is Catwoman?

Colin: Haven't you been listening to a word I've
been saying?

Word list
① ditch [dɪtʃ] v.【俚】甩開
② feline [ˋfilaɪn] adj. 像貓一樣的

柯林：你看過《貓女》這部電影嗎？

凱特：沒有，還沒看。好看嗎？

柯林：好看，實際上還滿有趣的。情節不錯，而且又有莎朗·史東。

凱特：喔，她不錯。她現在一定變得有點老了。

柯林：是啊，可是她看起來還是很漂亮。

凱特：所以這部電影在講什麼？

柯林：哦，它是在講一個女的被人謀殺，因為她在自己所服務的化妝品公司裡發現了一些秘密。可是後來她化身成為一隻貓。

凱特：嗄？

柯林：我知道，聽我說。後來她決定報仇，於是便公佈公司的秘密並殺了老闆。不過，她必須先找出她真正的貓本性。到最後，她跟莎朗·史東那個角色大戰了一場，她才是公司背後真正的危險人物。老闆其實是她殺的，而且老闆還是她老公。然後她試圖陷害貓女，說人是她殺的，所以每個人都覺得貓女很壞。

凱特：我懂了。嫁給老闆的是貓女嗎？

柯林：不是，嫁給老闆的是莎朗·史東那個角色。他對她很壞，所以她才殺了他。我說到哪兒了？對了，在此同時，貓女愛上了調查老闆謀殺案的警察。最後，為了順從她的貓本性，她拋棄了那位警察。

凱特：等一下，我搞亂了。是警察殺了老闆嗎？

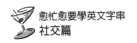

柯林：不是，是莎朗‧史東殺的。

凱特：那莎朗‧史東是貓女嗎？

柯林：你有在聽我說的任何一個字嗎？

Colin: Did you hear what happened to Mike in Accounting?

Kate: No. What?

Colin: He got arrested on Friday night and spent the night in jail.

Kate: <u>Really</u>? <u>What happened</u>?

Colin: Well, it was all a big mistake, actually. He got home on Friday night really late, and apparently he'd been out drinking with some clients, so he was really drunk.

Kate: Was he out with the guys from the bank?

Colin: <u>Yes</u>, I think so.

Kate: Oh, yeah, they always get really drunk.

Colin: <u>Well, anyway</u>, he'd somehow lost his wallet and his house keys, so he couldn't get in. He lives alone, you know.

Kate: Oh? I thought he lived with his wife.

Colin: No, she left him last year.

Kate: <u>Really</u>? Do you know why?

Colin: Hang on, let me finish telling you what happened. <u>Where was I</u>?

Kate: He lost his wallet and keys.

Colin: Oh yes, <u>well</u>, he tried to climb in through the

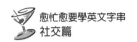
bathroom window, but apparently he slipped and broke the glass with his foot. The neighbors heard him and thought a robbery was in progress, so they called the police.

Kate: <u>Oh, no</u>.

Colin: <u>Right</u>. So when the cops arrived, they didn't believe his story—you know, he lost his wallet so he had no ID, the neighbors were new and didn't know him, and so he couldn't get the police to believe his story. So they arrested him and put him in a cell until the morning.

Kate: <u>So then what happened</u>?

Colin: <u>Well</u>, when he sobered[1] up, he called someone from work to come and bail[2] him out.

Kate: <u>Well</u>, that's a bit of a tricky situation.

Colin: <u>Yeah</u>. Tell me about it.

Word list
① sober [ˋsobə] v. 酒醒;清醒
② bail [bel] v. 保釋

中譯

柯林：你有聽說財務部的 Mike 出事了嗎？

凱特：不知道。他怎麼了？

柯林：他星期五晚上被捕，而且被關了一個晚上。

凱特：不會吧。到底是怎麼回事？

柯林：哦，其實一切都是很大的錯誤。他星期五晚上很晚才回家，他顯然是和幾個客戶出去喝了幾杯，而且喝得爛醉。

凱特：他是跟銀行的那些人出去嗎？

柯林：我想是吧。

凱特：喔，是啊，他們老是喝得爛醉。

柯林：哦，反正他就是弄丟了錢包跟家裡的鑰匙，所以沒辦法進門。你也知道，他是一個人住。

凱特：真的喔。我以為他跟老婆住在一起。

柯林：並沒有，她去年離開他了。

凱特：喔，真的嗎？你知道是為什麼嗎？

柯林：等等，先讓我把事情的經過說完。我說到哪兒了？

凱特：他弄丟了錢包跟鑰匙。

柯林：喔，對。他想要從浴室的窗戶爬進去，可是顯然滑了一跤，腳也踢破了玻璃。鄰居聽到了聲音，以為有人闖空門，於是叫警察來。

凱特：噢，不會吧。

柯林：是啊，結果警察來了以後，並不相信他的說法。你也知道，他弄丟了錢包，所以身上沒有身分證。鄰居是新來

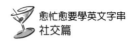

的，也不認識他，所以他沒辦法讓警察相信他的說法。
結果警察就逮捕了他，並把他關在拘留所裡，直到隔天
早上。

凱特：結果後來又怎麼了？

柯林：哦，等他醒來以後，他便打電話請公司的人來保他出
去。

凱特：哦，這種情況不太好處理。

柯林：是啊，我知道。

Part 4
餐廳中的談話

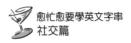

MP3 25

1 邀請
Inviting

Hungry?
餓了嗎？

Are you hungry?
你餓了嗎？

How hungry are you?
你有多餓？

Have you eaten?
你吃過飯了嗎？

Shall we go get something to eat?
我們要不要去吃點東西？

Would you like to have breakfast/lunch/ dinner/a snack?
你想要吃早餐／午餐／晚餐／點心嗎？

Would you like breakfast/lunch/dinner/a snack?
你想要吃早餐／午餐／晚餐／點心嗎？

Would you like something to eat?

你想要吃點東西嗎？

We'd like to invite you to dinner.

我們想邀請你吃晚餐。

We'd like to invite you to have dinner with us.

我們想邀請你和我們共進晚餐。

We'd be very happy if you'd have dinner with us.

如果你能和我們共進晚餐，我們會很高興。

 教父小叮嚀

◉ 這些字串是以「非正式→正式」的順序列出：第一個字串最不正
式；最後一個字串最正式。可依你與對方關係的親疏來決定使用哪
一個字串。

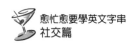
MP3 26

2 接受
Accepting

Sure, why not?
當然，有何不可？

That'd be great, thanks.
那太棒了，謝謝。

That would be lovely. Thank you.
真貼心，謝謝。

That's very kind of you. Thank you.
你真好，謝謝。

 教父小叮嚀

● 這些字串是以「非正式→正式」的順序列出：第一個字串最不正式；最後一個字串最正式。可依你與對方關係的親疏來決定使用哪一個字串。

3 拒絕
Rejecting

Another time perhaps? I've got to dash.[1]

也許下一次吧？我趕時間。

Could we do it another time?

我們下次好嗎？

That'd be great, thanks, but unfortunately + clause.

那太棒了，謝謝，只可惜……。

例 That'd be great, thanks, but unfortunately I have an urgent meeting tonight.

那太棒了，謝謝，只可惜我今晚有一場緊急的會議。

That'd be great, thanks, but unfortunately I have a flight to catch.

那太棒了，謝謝，只可惜我得趕飛機。

That would be lovely, but unfortunately + clause.

那真貼心，只可惜……。

Word list
① dash [dæʃ] v. 匆忙離開

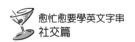
例 That would be lovely, but unfortunately I have to take my daughter to the dentist.

那真貼心，只可惜我得帶我女兒去看牙醫。

That would be lovely, but unfortunately I've got another client to visit today.

那真貼心，只可惜我今天要去拜訪另一名客戶。

 教父小叮嚀

● 這些字串是以「非正式 → 正式」的順序列出：第一個字串最不正式；最後一個字串最正式。可依你與對方關係的親疏來決定使用哪一個字串。

● 拒絕邀請時儘量委婉，不要直接說 no。說明拒絕的理由會更得體。

4 詢問菜單上的餐點——客人
Asking about something on the menu—the guest

What's the n.p.?

……是什麼？

例 What's the apricot confit?

杏桃凍是什麼？

What's the salmon terrine?

鮭魚派是什麼？

Can you tell me about the n.p.?

可以麻煩你介紹一下……嗎？

例 Can you tell me about the rack of lamb?

可以麻煩你介紹一下羊肋排嗎？

Can you tell me about the steamed haddock?[1]

可以麻煩你介紹一下清蒸黑線鱈嗎？

What does "n.p." mean?

「……」是什麼意思？

Word list

① haddock [ˋhædək] *n.* 黑線鱈

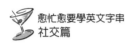

例 What does "plat du jour" mean?

「今日特餐」是什麼意思？

What does "suppa del giorno" mean?

「每日一湯」是什麼意思？

Is it spicy?

它會辣嗎？

Is it oily?

它會油嗎？

Is it meat?

這是肉嗎？

Is it low-fat?

這是低脂的嗎？

Is it salty?

它會鹹嗎？

Does it have n.p. in it? I'm allergic¹ to n.p.

這裡面有……嗎？我對……過敏。

例 Does it have nuts in it? I'm allergic to nuts.

這裡面有核果嗎？我對核果類過敏。

Word list
① allergic [əˋlədʒɪk] *adj.* 過敏的

Does it have seafood in it? I'm allergic to seafood.
這裡面有海鮮嗎？我對海鮮過敏。

What are you having?
你要吃什麼？

What can you recommend?
你會推薦什麼？

What's good here?
這裡什麼東西不錯？

Why don't you just order for both of us?
你何不幫我們兩個人一起點？

What does it come with?
它的配菜是什麼？

 教父小叮嚀

- Is it spicy? 也可說成 Is it hot?，但這樣可能會使對方混淆。因為 hot 有「燙」、「辣」兩種意思。
- 大部分的菜單只會註明主菜是肉還是魚，蔬菜和馬鈴薯算是配菜。 所以你可以用 What does it come with? 來問問搭配的配菜是什麼。

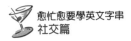
MP3 29

 推薦餐點——主人
Recommending something on the menu—the host

The n.p. is very good here.

這裡的……很好吃。

例 The steak is very good here.

這裡的牛排很好吃。

The seafood is very good here.

這裡的海鮮很好吃。

You should try the n.p.

你應該試試……。

例 You should try the sweet and sour pork.

你應該試試糖醋排骨。

You should try the meatloaf.

你應該試試烤肉條。

Try some n.p.

試一些……。

例 Try some red wine.

試一些紅酒吧。

Try some bacon.

試一些培根。

Have you tried n.p.?

你吃過……嗎？

例 Have you tried frog's legs?

你吃過田雞腿嗎？

Have you tried deep fried Camembert?

你吃過炸卡蒙貝爾乳酪嗎？

You might want to try the n.p. It's a local delicacy.[1]

你也許會想試試……。它是當地美食。

例 You might want to try the crab soup. It's a local delicacy.

你也許會想試試螃蟹湯。它是當地的美食。

You might want to try the steamed trout. It's a local delicacy.

你也許會想試試清蒸鱒魚。它是當地的美食。

You could try n.p.

你可以試試……。

Word list

① delicacy [ˈdɛləkəsɪ] n. 佳餚

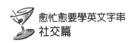
例 You could try the ravioli.[1]

你可以試試義大利方餃。

You could try the lentil[2] stew.

你可以試試德國扁豆湯。

How about n.p.?

……如何？

例 How about some wine?

葡萄酒如何？

How about a steak?

牛排如何？

Would you like the n.p.?

你想吃……嗎？

例 Would you like the garlic snails?

你想吃蒜香蝸牛嗎？

Would you like the goat's cheese?

你想吃羊奶乳酪嗎？

Word list
① ravioli [ˌrævɪˋolɪ] *n.* 義式水餃
② lentil [ˋlɛntɪl] *n.* 小扁豆

Would you like some n.p.?

你想來一點……嗎？

例 Would you like some wine?

你想來一點葡萄酒嗎？

Would you like some vegetables?

你想來一點蔬菜嗎？

Would you like me to order for you?

你想要我幫你點菜嗎？

It sounds horrible, but it's actually really good.

它聽起來有點恐怖，不過真的好吃極了。

It's a little adj.

它有點……。

例 It's a little oily.

它有點油。

It's a little salty.

它有點鹹。

It might be too adj. for you.

它對你來說可能太……了。

例 It might be too salty for you.

它對你來說可能太鹹了。

It might be too strange for you.

它對你來說可能太奇特了。

 教父小叮嚀

◉ 如果你覺得客人可能誤點他不喜歡的餐點,你可以說: It's a little ....
或 It might be too ... for you. 來提醒對方。

6 點餐
Ordering something on the menu

I'll have the n.p.
我要……。

例 I'll have the fish.
我要魚。

I'll have the beef stew.
我要燉牛肉。

Can I have the n.p.?
給我……好嗎？

例 Can I have the ramen?[1]
給我拉麵好嗎？

Can I have the seafood curry?
給我海鮮咖哩好嗎？

Not too spicy/salty/sweet, please.
麻煩不要太辣／鹹／甜。

Part
4

餐廳中的談話

Word list
① ramen [ˈrɑmɛn] *n.* 拉麵

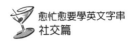
I'd like the n.p.

我要……。

例 I'd like the pumkin soup.

我要南瓜湯。

I'd like the tomato salad.

我要蕃茄沙拉。

For my starter,[1] I'll have the n.p.

我要……當開胃菜。

例 For my starter, I'll have the soup.

我要湯當開胃菜。

For my starter, I'll have the salmon pate.[2]

我要鮭魚醬當開胃菜。

For my main course, I'd like the n.p.

我要……當主菜。

例 For my main course, I'd like the steak.

我要牛排當主菜。

For my main course, I'd like the spaghetti.[3]

我要義大利肉醬麵當主菜。

Word list

① starter [ˋstɑrtə] *n.* （套餐中的）第一道菜

② pate [pɑˋte] *n.* 肉醬

③ spaghetti [spəˋgɛtɪ] *n.* 義大利麵

For dessert, I'll have the n.p.

我要……當甜點。

例 For dessert, I'll have the cheesecake.

我要乳酪蛋糕當甜點。

For dessert, I'll have the sorbet.[1]

我要果汁冰砂當甜點。

That's it.

就這樣。

That'll do it.

這樣就夠了。

That'll do it for us. Thank you.

我們這樣就夠了。謝謝你。

教父小叮嚀

● 點餐完畢，就可對服務生說：That's it.、That'll do it. 或 That'll do it for us. Thank you.。

Word list

① sorbet [ˋsɔrbɪt] *n.* 果汁冰砂

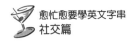
MP3 31

7 開始、結束、抱怨和詢問
Starting, ending, complaining, and asking

Excuse me.
不好意思。（用來吸引服務生的注意）

Can we have the menu, please?
可以給我們菜單嗎？

Can we have the check, please?
可以給我們帳單嗎？

Can I have the bill, please?
可以給我帳單嗎？

Can I have the wine list, please?
可以給我酒單嗎？

Can you tell me what the specials are, please?
可以請你介紹一下特餐嗎？

Can you tell me what the soup of the day is, please?
可以請你介紹一下「每日一湯」嗎？

Can you tell me what the n.p. is, please?
可以請你介紹一下……嗎？

例 Can you tell me what the terrine is, please?

可以請你介紹一下法國派嗎？

Can you tell me what the lunch special is, please?

可以請你介紹一下中午的特餐嗎？

I'm sorry, but there's something wrong with my food.

對不起，但是我的食物有問題。

I'm sorry, but this is not what I ordered.

對不起，但是這不是我點的東西。

I'm sorry, but we're still waiting for the n.p.

對不起，但是我們還在等……。

例 I'm sorry, but we're still waiting for the soup.

對不起，但是我們還在等湯。

I'm sorry, but we're still waiting for the prawns.

對不起，但是我們還在等蝦子。

I'm sorry, can you explain this item on the bill, please?

對不起，可以請你解釋一下帳單上的這個項目嗎？

I'm sorry, but I don't think this is what we ordered.

對不起，但是我不覺得這是我們點的東西。

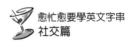

對話範例

Sandra: Well, Brad, that was a very productive meeting, I thought. You had some really great ideas in there!

Brad: Really? Well, thanks for saying so.

Sandra: No, I mean it. Look, <u>are you hungry? Shall we go get something to eat?</u>

Brad: <u>Sure. Why not?</u>

Sandra: OK, well, let me just get my coat and we'll go to the diner[1] around the corner.

Brad: OK.

Word list
① diner [ˋdaɪnɚ] *n.* 餐車式的速食餐廳

中譯

珊德拉：嘿，布萊德，我覺得這次開會的成果豐碩，你在裏頭
　　　　提出的那些點子真棒！

布萊德：真的嗎？謝謝你的誇獎。

珊德拉：不，我是說真的。你餓了嗎？我們要不要去吃點東
　　　　西？

布萊德：當然好呀！

珊德拉：好，那我拿一下外套，我們去轉角的館子吃飯。

布萊德：好。

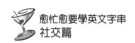
②

Colin: That was a very interesting presentation, Ms. Wong. My colleagues and I are very impressed with your proposal.

Ms. Wong: Oh, no, surely. Your ideas were very interesting as well.

Colin: To show our appreciation for your hard work, we'd like to invite you to have dinner with us.

Ms. Wong: Oh, that would be lovely. Thank you.

Colin: Excellent. Have you had French food before?

Ms. Wong: Oh, yes. Marvelous[1] ....

柯　林：王小姐，這場簡報很有趣。我跟我同事對妳的提案都印象深刻。

王小姐：喔，真不敢當。你們的點子也很有趣。

柯　林：為了答謝妳的辛苦付出，我們想請妳共進晚餐。

王小姐：喔，你們真貼心，謝謝。

柯　林：太好了。妳吃過法國菜嗎？

王小姐：喔，吃過，味道很棒……

Word list

① marvelous [ˋmɑrvləs] *adj.* 很棒的；出色的

③

Kate: Well, I'm getting really hungry. I think we should take a break and come back to this item after lunch. <u>Shall we go get something to eat?</u>

Brad: <u>Sure. Why not?</u> Do you know somewhere cheap and quick?

凱　特：欸，我真的好餓。我想我們應該先休息一下，等吃完午飯再回來繼續這個項目。我們要不要去吃點東西？

布萊德：當然好啊。你知道有什麼便宜又快的地方嗎？

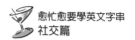

④

Sandra: It's getting rather late. Can I suggest that we stop at this point and perhaps regroup tomorrow? I think we could all do with some rest. Mr. Wang, we'd like to invite you to dinner.

Mr. Wang: That would be lovely, but unfortunately I need to get back to my hotel as I'm expecting a call from my wife. Perhaps we could meet for breakfast?

中譯

珊德拉：時間很晚了，我想我們能不能到此為止，也許明天再碰頭？我覺得我們都可以休息一下。王先生，我們想請你吃晚餐。

王先生：那真貼心，只可惜我要回飯店等我老婆的電話。也許我們可以一起吃早餐？

Colin: My God! Will you look at the time! It's after 8:00! My wife will kill me. Kate, <u>are you hungry</u>? Do you want something to eat before you go back to your hotel?

Kate: <u>Could we do it another time?</u> I'm a little tired. I've still got jet lag from my flight. How about tomorrow or the next day?

柯林：天啊！你看時間，已經過八點了！我老婆會殺了我。凱特，你餓不餓？你想在回飯店前吃點東西嗎？

凱特：改天好嗎？我有點累。我還有點飛行的時差問題。明天或後天如何？

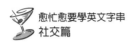

⑥

Mr. Wang: Well, Kate, I hope you like it here. This is my favourite restaurant in Taipei. It reminds me of my youth when I traveled around Europe.

Kate: It looks wonderful. Very authentic.[1]

Mr. Wang: The chef[2] trained in Florence. <u>The pasta is very good here.</u>

Kate: OK. So, <u>what can you recommend?</u>

Mr. Wang: Umm... <u>You should try the mushroom fettuccine.</u> It's really good.

Kate: <u>Is it salty?</u>

Mr. Wang: Not at all. It has a very delicate flavor.

Kate: <u>What does "Zuppa del giorno" mean?</u> I'm sorry I don't know how to pronounce that.

Mr. Wang: Oh, that means soup of the day. I'll ask the waiter what they have today. <u>Have you tried mussels[3] cooked the Italian way?</u> They're really delicious.

Kate: No. I'll try them. Sounds good.

Word list
① authentic [ɔ`θɛntɪk] *adj.* 真實的；可信的
② chef [ʃɛf] *n.* 廚師
③ mussel [`mʌsl] *n.* 淡菜

中譯

王先生：對了，凱特，希望你喜歡這裡。這是我在台北最喜歡
　　　　的餐館，它讓我想起我在歐洲旅遊的年輕時代。

凱　特：看起來很棒，就像真的歐洲餐廳一樣。

王先生：大廚是在佛羅倫斯學藝，這裡的義大利麵很好吃。

凱　特：好。所以你可以推薦一下嗎？

王先生：呣，你應該試試香菇麵，味道很棒。

凱　特：它會很鹹嗎？

王先生：一點都不會。它的味道很清淡。

凱　特：Zuppa del giorno 是什麼意思？抱歉，我不曉得
　　　　要怎麼唸。

王先生：喔，那是每日一湯的意思。我會問服務生今天是什麼
　　　　湯。你吃過義大利式的淡菜嗎？它的味道很棒。

凱　特：沒吃過，那就試試看吧，聽起來不錯。

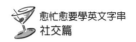

Mr. Wang: This looks wonderful, Kate.

Kate: Yes, it's very nice. All our foreign visitors enjoy it. The food is wonderfully well-prepared. Let me know if you need any help with the menu.

Mr. Wang: Thank you. Mmm. <u>Can you tell me about the terrine?</u>

Kate: Yes. A terrine is a kind of meat pate. It's meat turned into a paste. <u>It sounds horrible but actually it's really good.</u>

Mr. Wang: Mmm. Maybe another time.

Kate: <u>You could try the ravioli.</u> They are rather like your Chinese dumplings, and the sauce is delicious.

Mr. Wang: Sounds good. I think <u>I'll have the lamb for my main course.</u> <u>What does it come with?</u>

Kate: Well, you can have frites, which means French fries, or simple boiled potatoes.

Mr. Wang: I'll have the potatoes. <u>What are you having?</u>

Kate: I'm having my usual. I like the fish here. <u>Would you like some wine?</u>

Mr. Wang: Yes, please. <u>That would be lovely.</u>

中譯

王先生：凱特，這裡看起來很不錯。

凱　特：是啊，的確很棒。我們的外國客人一向都很喜歡，而且它的菜餚都經過精心烹調。假如你對菜單有什麼不了解的地方，請告訴我。

王先生：謝謝。嗯，可以麻煩妳介紹一下 terrine 嗎？

凱　特：好的。Terrine 是一種肉餅，也就是把肉變成餅。它聽起來有點恐怖，不過真的好吃極了。

王先生：嗯，也許下次吧。

凱　特：你可以試試 ravioli。它很像是中國的水餃，而且醬料很好吃。

王先生：聽起來不錯。我想我的主菜就吃羊肉好了。它的副餐是什麼？

凱　特：哦，你可以吃 frites，也就是薯條，或是簡單的水煮馬鈴薯。

王先生：那我吃馬鈴薯好了。妳要吃什麼呢？

凱　特：我還是老樣子，我喜歡吃這裡的魚。你要喝點酒嗎？

王先生：好啊。妳真貼心。

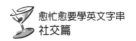

⑧

Mr. Wang: <u>Can we have a menu, please.</u>

Waiter: Of course, sir. Here you are.

(a few minutes later, the waiter returns)

Waiter: Are you ready to order, sir?

Mr. Wang: Yes. Kate, please go first.

Kate: All right. <u>I'll have the mussels</u>, and then <u>I'll have the fettucine.</u>

Waiter: Would you like a main course, madame?

Kate: No, I don't think so. I think the pasta will be enough for me.

Waiter: And you, sir?

Mr. Wang: <u>Can you tell me what the soup of the day is?</u>

Waiter: Yes. It's minestrone soup. That's a rich tomato and vegetable soup.

Mr. Wang: OK, I'll have that, but not too salty, please. And <u>for my main course I'll have the veal.</u> <u>That's it.</u> We might order some of your excellent tiramisu later.

Waiter: Very good, sir.

王先生：可以請你給我們菜單嗎？

服務生：沒問題，先生。請看。

（幾分鐘過後，服務生回來了）

服務生：你們要點餐了嗎，先生？

王先生：凱特，請妳先點。

凱　特：好。我要淡菜，然後我還要麵。

服務生：小姐，您要主菜嗎？

凱　特：我想不用了。我想我吃麵就夠了。

服務生：先生，您呢？

王先生：你能告訴我今天的湯是什麼嗎？

服務生：好的，是蔬菜濃湯，也就是有番茄和蔬菜的濃湯。

王先生：好，那我點那個，不過麻煩不要太鹹。我的主菜要小牛肉，就這樣。我們等一下可能會點一些你們這邊很棒的提拉米蘇。

服務生：太好了，先生。

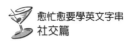
⑨

Waiter:	Would you like to order some wine first, madame?
Kate:	Yes. <u>Can I have the wine list, please?</u>
Waiter:	Here you are, madame.

(a few minutes later, the waiter returns)

Waiter:	Would you like to order now?
Kate:	Yes. Mr. Wang, what would you like?
Mr. Wang:	OK. <u>For my starter I'd like the ravioli</u>, followed by the lamb for my main course. And <u>can I have the potatoes boiled</u>, not fried, please.
Waiter:	Of course, sir. Madame?
Kate:	Mmm. <u>Can you tell me what the specials are, please?</u>
Waiter:	Today we have beef bourguignon as the entree and escargots for hors d'oeuvres.
Kate:	Oh, Mr. Wang, would you like to try snails?
Mr. Wang:	Sure.
Waiter:	So would you like to change the ravioli to snails, sir? Or have both?
Kate:	Why don't we have one dish of snails between us to share? Then you can try the ravioli and the snails.

Mr. Wang: Good idea.

Waiter: All right. And for your main course, madame?

Kate: <u>I'll have the beef</u>, and a soup du jour to start with.

Waiter: Very good, madame.

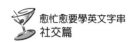

服務生：小姐，您要先點杯酒嗎？

凱　特：好。可以麻煩你給我酒單嗎？

服務生：小姐，請過目。

（幾分鐘過後，服務生回來了）

服務生：您現在要點了嗎？

凱　特：好。王先生，你想要什麼？

王先生：好。開胃菜我要義大利餃子，接下來的主菜則要羊肉。我可以點水煮馬鈴薯嗎？麻煩不要用炸的。

服務生：當然可以，先生。小姐呢？

凱　特：姆。可以麻煩你介紹一下特餐嗎？

服務生：今天我們有勃艮第牛肉當主菜，開胃菜則是蝸牛。

凱　特：噢，王先生，你想試試蝸牛嗎？

王先生：哦，好啊。

服務生：先生，所以您要把義大利餃子換成蝸牛，還是兩個都要？

凱　特：我們何不點一份蝸牛一起吃？這樣你就可以同時吃到義大利餃子和蝸牛了。

王先生：好主意。

服務生：好的。小姐，您的主菜要什麼？

凱　特：我要牛肉，然後先來個濃湯。

服務生：太好了，小姐。

Part 5
宴會中的談話

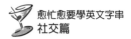

MP3 33

1 自我介紹
Introducing yourself

Hello, ...
嗨，……。

例 Hello, Kate.
嗨，凱特。

Hello, Mike.
嗨，麥克。

Hello. I'm ....
嗨，我是……。

例 Hello. I'm Kate.
嗨，我是凱特。

Hello. I'm Mike.
嗨，我是麥克。

Hello, my name's ....
嗨，我叫……。

例 Hello, my name's Kate.
嗨，我叫凱特。

Hello, my name's Mike.

嗨，我叫麥克。

I'm ..., by the way. / By the way, I'm ....

對了，我是……。／對了，我是……。

例 I'm Kate, by the way.

對了，我是凱特。

By the way, I'm Mike.

對了，我是麥克。

Pleased to meet you.

很高興認識你。

Pleased to meet you, too.

我也很高興認識你。

It's a pleasure.

很榮幸。

It's a pleasure to meet you.

很榮幸認識你。

It's a pleasure to meet you, too.

我也很榮幸認識你。

How do you do?

你好嗎？

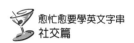
Nice to meet you.

很高興認識你。

Nice to meet you, too.

我也很高興認識你。

教父小叮嚀

◉ Nice to meet you. / Nice to meet you, too. ; Pleased to meet you. /
Pleased to meet you, too. 這些字串是成對出現，當說話者 A 說第一句
時，說話者 B 就要說第二句。這些字串在正式和非正式的場合都適
用。

2 介紹別人
Introducing someone else

X, I'd like to introduce you to Y.
……，我想要介紹你跟……認識。

例 Mike, I'd like to introduce you to Kate.

麥克，我想要介紹你跟凱特認識。

Kate, I'd like to introduce you to Mike.

凱特，我想要介紹妳跟麥克認識。

X, let me introduce you to Y.
……，讓我介紹你跟……認識。

例 Mike, let me introduce you to Kate.

麥克，讓我介紹你跟凱特認識。

Kate, let me introduce you to Mike.

凱特，讓我介紹妳跟麥克認識。

X, I want you to meet Y.
……，我想要你見見……。

例 Mike, I want you to meet Kate.

麥克，我想要你見見凱特。

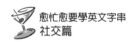
Kate, I want you to meet Mike.

凱特，我想要妳見見麥克。

X, have you met Y?

……，你見過……嗎？

例 Mike, have you met Kate?

麥克，你見過凱特嗎？

Kate, have you met Mike?

凱特，妳見過麥克嗎？

X, do you know Y?

……，你認識……嗎？

例 Mike, do you know Kate?

麥克，你認識凱特嗎？

Kate, do you know Mike?

凱特，妳認識麥克嗎？

X, this is Y.

……，這位是……。

例 Mike, this is Kate.

麥克，這位是凱特。

Kate, this is Mike.

凱特，這位是麥克。

X, Y.

……，……。

例 Mike, Kate.

麥克，凱特。

Kate, Mike.

凱特，麥克。

Have you met X?

你見過……嗎？

例 Have you met Mike?

你見過麥克嗎？

Have you met Kate?

你見過凱特嗎？

Do you know X?

你認識……嗎？

例 Do you know Mike?

你認識麥克嗎？

Do you know Kate?

你認識凱特嗎？

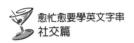
Do you two know each other?

你們兩個彼此認識嗎？

Have you two met?

你們兩個見過嗎？

教父小叮嚀

◉ 字串中的 X 和 Y 指的是「人名」。

3 介紹基本資訊
Giving basic information

He/She's in n.p.

他／她是做……的。

例 She's in accounting.

她是做會計的。

He's in advertising.

他是做廣告的。

I'm in n.p.

我是做……的。

例 I'm in sales.

我是做業務的。

I'm in the technology industry.

我是做科技業的。

He/She works in n.p.

他／她在……工作。

例 She works in finance.

她在金融業工作。

He works in marketing.

他在行銷業工作。

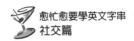

He/She works for n.p.

他／她在……服務。

例 She works for IBM.

她在 IBM 服務。

He works for HP.

他在 HP 服務。

He/She is based[1] in n.p.

他／她在……工作。

例 She's based in Shanghai.

她在上海工作。

He's based in Hsinchu.

他在新竹工作。

He/She works out of n.p.

他／她在……工作。

例 She works out of Taipei.

她在台北工作。

He works out of Banqiao.

他在板橋工作。

Word list

① base [bes] *v.* 以……為根據地

He/She has his/her own n.p.

他／她開了一家自己的……。

例 She has her own advertising company.

她開了一家自己的廣告公司。

He has his own construction firm.

他開了一家自己的營建事務所。

He/She runs his/her own n.p.

他／她經營自己的……。

例 She runs her own design company.

她經營自己的設計公司。

He runs his own trading operation.

他經營自己的貿易事業。

I work in n.p.

我在……工作。

例 I work in advertising.

我在廣告業工作。

I work in a law office.

我在一間法律事務所工作。

I work for n.p.

我在……服務。

例 I work for an international trading company.
　　我在一間國際貿易公司服務。

　　I work for Yoyodyne, Ltd.
　　我在友友戴恩服務。

I'm based in n.p.

我在……工作。

例 I'm based in Taiwan.
　　我在台灣工作。

　　I'm based in China.
　　我在中國工作。

I work out of n.p.

我在……工作。

例 I work out of Hsinchu.
　　我在新竹工作。

　　I work out of Taoyuan.
　　我在桃園工作。

I have my own n.p.

我開了一家自己的……。

例 I have my own photography studio.
　　我開了一家自己的攝影工作室。

I have my own financial consultancy.

我開了一家自己的財務諮詢公司。

I run my own n.p.

我經營自己的……。

例 I run my own graphic design service.

我經營自己的圖像設計服務。

I run my own trading company.

我經營自己的貿易公司。

 教父小叮嚀

● 在此部分的字串中，n.p. 指的可能是商業領域（例如：會計）、公司名稱（例如：友友戴恩）、地名（例如：北京）或是公司類型（例如：貿易公司、銀行）。可以搭配例句記住字串用法。

● work out of 指的是在某處工作，但有外派和經常出差的可能。

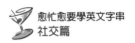

MP3 36

4 傳述
Passing it on

According to sb., + clause.

聽某人說，……。

例 According to the news, they are going to merge.

聽新聞說，他們要合併了。

According to Colin, the stock price is very high at the moment.

聽柯林說，股價目前非常高。

According to the grapevine, + clause.

有謠言說，……。

例 According to the grapevine, Mary has already left her job.

有謠言說，瑪麗已經辭掉她的工作。

According to the grapevine, they are in financial difficulties.

有謠言說，他們財務有困難。

Aren't they supposed to be Ving?

他們不是應該要……嗎？

例 Aren't they supposed to be moving to Shanghai?

他們不是應該要搬到上海嗎？

Aren't they supposed to be merging?

它們不是應該要合併嗎？

Aren't you supposed to be Ving?

你不是應該要……嗎？

例 Aren't you supposed to be changing jobs next week?

你不是應該下週要換工作嗎？

Aren't you supposed to be working on that big project?

你不是應該要處理那個大案子嗎？

From what I hear, + clause.

據我所知，……。

例 From what I hear, they are having an affair.

據我所知，他們有一腿。

From what I hear, they are not doing very well these days.

據我所知，他們最近情況不太好。

From what I ('ve) heard, + clause.

據我所知，……。

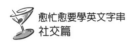
例 From what I heard, the new boss is very strict.

據我所知，新老闆很嚴格。

From what I've heard, that's not a good company to work for.

據我所知，那不是一家任職的好公司。

Haven't you heard?

你還沒聽說嗎？

Have you heard the news?

你聽說那個消息了嗎？

Have you heard the latest gossip?

你聽說最新的八卦了嗎？

I hear that + clause.

我聽說……。

例 I hear that they are going to close down some branches.

我聽說他們打算要關掉一些分公司。

I hear that they are getting a divorce.

我聽說他們要離婚。

I hear you're thinking of Ving?

我聽說你在考慮……？

例 I hear you're thinking of moving to the US?

我聽說你在考慮搬到美國？

I hear you're thinking of doing an MBA?

我聽說你在考慮去念 MBA？

I heard it through the grapevine that + clause.

我聽到謠言說……。

例 I heard it through the grapevine that they are recruiting[1] at the moment.

我聽到謠言說他們目前在招募新人。

I heard it through the grapevine that they are getting married.

我聽到謠言說他們要結婚了。

I heard that + clause.

我聽說……。

例 I heard that she was very ill.

我聽說她病得非常重。

I heard that he got fired.

我聽說他被開除了。

Word list
① recruit [rɪ`krut] *v.* 徵募新人

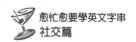
I read somewhere that + clause.

我從某個地方讀到……。

例 I read somewhere that the company was in trouble.

我從某個地方讀到這家公司有麻煩了。

I read somewhere that the market was shrinking.[1]

我從某個地方讀到市場正在萎縮。

I thought everyone knew.

我以為大家都知道。

I thought it was common knowledge.

我以為這件事大家都知道。

I understand (that) + clause.

我得知……。

例 I understand they are having financial problems.

我得知他們現在有財務問題。

I understand that the government regulations are very strict.

我得知政府規範非常嚴格。

I'm not one to gossip, but + clause.

我不愛說長道短，但是……。

Word list

① shrink [ʃrɪŋk] *v.* 收縮；縮小

例 I'm not one to gossip, but they have a thing going on![1]

我不愛說長道短，但是他們之間有曖昧！

I'm not one to gossip, but she got fired for embezzling[2] money from the company!

我不愛說長道短，但是她因為盜用公款而被開除了。

It appears that + clause.

看來……。

例 It appears that the board dismissed[3] the CEO.

看來董事會開除了執行長。

It appears that the share price was manipulated.[4]

看來股價被操控了。

It seems that + clause.

……似乎……。

Word list

① have a thing going on 有一腿；有曖昧（= have an affair）

② embezzle [ɪmˋbɛzl] v. 盜用（公款）

③ dismiss [dɪsˋmɪs] v. 解僱；遣散

④ manipulate [məˋnɪpjə,let] v. 操縱

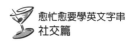
例 It seems that things are always going wrong in that company.

那家公司似乎總是出問題。

It seems that they are going to lay off two thousand people!

他們似乎要裁掉兩千人！

It sounds as if + clause.

聽起來好像……。

例 It sounds as if they are in serious trouble.

聽起來好像他們碰上了大麻煩。

It sounds as if it's not a good place to work.

聽起來好像這不是個工作的好地方。

Rumor has it that + clause.

有傳聞說，……。

例 Rumor has it that things are not going well there.

有傳聞說，那裡的狀況不太好。

Rumor has it that she is a terrible and totally incompetent manager.

有傳聞說，她是一個既差勁又毫無能力可言的經理。

Someone told me + clause.

有人跟我說，……。

例 Someone told me that they are suing her.

有人跟我說，他們要告她。

Someone told me that you are leaving (the company).

有人跟我說，你要離開（公司）了。

They say + clause.

有人說……。

例 They say things in the company are not going well.

有人說公司的狀況不太好。

They say it's a very unpleasant situation.

有人說這是個令人非常不舒服的情形。

 教父小叮嚀

● 注意字串中動詞 hear、think、read、seem、appear、sound、say、tell 等的用法。這些動詞都在說明你所說的話不代表你的意見，只是轉述其他來源的消息。

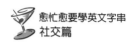

MP3 37

5 保密
Keeping it secret

Don't tell anyone, but + clause.
別告訴任何人,但是……。

例 Don't tell anyone, but I think they are having a fling![1]

別告訴任何人,但是我覺得他們有一腿!

Don't tell anyone, but I think Colin fancies Kate!

別告訴任何人,但是我覺得柯林喜歡凱特!

I don't want this to get out.
我不想要這件事情傳出去。

This is just between you and me.
這件事只能你知我知。

I won't mention any names, but + clause.
我不會指名道姓,但是……。

Word list
① have a fling 有一腿 (= have an affair)

例 I won't mention any names, but Brad told me something shocking yesterday!

我不會指名道姓，但是昨天布萊德告訴我一件讓人震驚的事！

I won't mention any names, but Alice and you know who are living together!

我不會指名道姓，但是你也明白愛麗絲和某人住在一起！

If word gets out that + clause ...

如果……的風聲走漏出去，……。

例 If word gets out that our products are unsafe, we'll be in big trouble.

如果我們產品不安全的風聲走漏出去，我們麻煩就大了。

If word gets out that our profits are down, the share price will collapse.[1]

如果我們利潤下跌的風聲走漏出去，股價會崩盤。

It's all a big secret.

這可是個大祕密。

Just between ourselves, + clause.

這件事只能我們自己知道，……。

Word list
① collapse [kə`læps] v. 暴跌

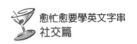

例 Just between ourselves, I think it's possible that we may go bankrupt.

這件事只能我們自己知道，我想我們可能會破產。

Just between ourselves, I don't like her at all.

這件事只能我們自己知道，我一點都不喜歡她。

Just between the two of us, + clause.

這件事只能我們兩個知道，……。

例 Just between the two of us, this is a really boring party.

這件事只能我們兩個知道，這個派對真是有夠無聊。

Just between the two of us, I think they could have spent more money on the food.

這件事只能我們兩個知道，我覺得他們大可多花一點錢在食物上。

Off the record, + clause.

別告訴別人，……。

例 Off the record, our profits are going to be very slim[1] this year.

別告訴別人，我們今年的利潤將會非常地微薄。

Word list
① slim [slɪm] *adj.* 微薄的

Off the record, the new product is totally unsafe!

別告訴別人，新產品一點都不安全！

This is just between us/ourselves, of course.

當然，這僅止於我們之間。

This is just between you and me, of course.

當然，這件事只能你知我知。

This is not to go any further, of course.

當然，這件事不能讓其他人知道。

This is not to go outside the room.

這件事不能從這個房間走漏出去。

Well, apparently, + clause.

嗯，似乎……。

例 Well, apparently, George is an alcoholic!

嗯，喬治似乎是個酒鬼。

Well, apparently, Alice has a serious drug problem!

嗯，愛麗絲似乎有很嚴重的藥物問題！

You didn't hear this from me.

你可不是從我這兒聽來的。

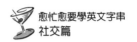
I didn't tell you this, but + clause.

別說是我說的，但是……。

例 I didn't tell you this, but Mike is going to be asked to leave at the end of the week.

別說是我說的，但是麥克被要求在這週結束前離開。

I didn't tell you this, but the marketing department is looking for a new manager.

別說是我說的，但是行銷部門正在找新的經理。

6 改變話題
Changing the topic

Can I just change the subject before I forget?

我可不可以在忘記前先改變一下話題？

Oh, by the way, + clause?

噢，對了，……？

例 Oh, by the way, are you going to the board meeting on Monday?

噢，對了，你要去星期一的董事會嗎？

Oh, by the way, how was your party last weekend? I forgot to ask you.

噢，對了，你上週末的派對如何？我忘了問你。

Oh, before I forget, + clause.

對了，在我忘記前先說一下，……。

例 Oh, before I forget, Sandra told me that she wants to give you the T&D account.

對了，在我忘記前先說一下，珊德拉告訴我她要把 T&D 這個客戶給你。

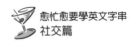
Oh, before I forget, Colin called while you were out this afternoon.

對了，在我忘記前先說一下，今天下午你外出時柯林打電話來過。

Oh, I meant to tell you earlier.

喔，我原本想早些告訴你。

Oh, about that ..., ...

對了，關於那個……，……。

例 Oh, about that restaurant you told me about, they already closed down!

對了，關於你告訴我的那間餐廳，他們已經關店了！

Oh, about that report you asked me to check, I gave it to Kate to finish.

對了，關於你要我檢查的那份報告，我把它交給凱特去完成了。

Oh, incidentally,[1] + clause.

噢，順便一提，……。

例 Oh, incidentally, we're having a get-together[2] on Sunday. Are you free to join us?

噢，順便一提，我們星期天要聚一聚。你有空參加嗎？

Word list
① incidentally [ˌɪnsəˋdɛntl̩ɪ] *adv.* 順便一提
② get-together [ˋgɛt təˌgɛðɚ] *n.* 聚會

Oh, incidentally, Brad wants to invite you to join the mountain climbing club.

噢,順便一提,布萊德要邀請你加入登山社。

Oh, that reminds me.

對了,那提醒了我。

Oh, while we're on the subject, + clause.

喔,既然我們聊到這件事,……。

例 Oh, while we're on the subject, I visited this fantastic church in Italy last summer.

對了,既然我們聊到這件事,我去年夏天造訪了這間美侖美奐的義大利教堂。

Oh, while we're on the subject, have you tried the new French restaurant on Fifth St.?

對了,既然我們聊到這件事,你試過第五街的那家新法國餐廳嗎?

Oh, you reminded me of something.

喔,你讓我想起一件事。

That reminds me of n.p.

那讓我想起……。

例 That reminds me of the movie I saw last night.

那讓我想起我昨晚看的電影。

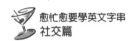
That reminds me of an article I read in
The Economist.

那讓我想起我在《經濟學人》看到的一篇文章。

Oh, by the way, listen to this.

噢，對了，聽聽這個。

Oh, by the way, + clause.

噢，對了，……。

例 Oh, by the way, give Alice a call when you get a
chance.

噢，對了，你有空的時候打個電話給愛麗絲。

Oh, by the way, the meeting has been changed
from Monday to Wednesday.

噢，對了，會議從星期一改到星期三了。

That reminds me of the time + clause.

那讓我想起……的時候。

例 That reminds me of the time I got lost in New York!

那讓我想起我在紐約迷路的時候！

That reminds me of the time I locked my keys in
my hotel room in Tokyo.

那讓我想起我在東京把鑰匙反鎖在旅館房間的時候。

On the subject of n.p., + clause.

說到……，……

例 On the subject of dogs, we gave my daughter a puppy for her seventh birthday.

說到狗，我們給了我女兒一隻小狗當作她七歲的生日禮物。

On the subject of wine, have you noticed how good the Merlot selection is lately?

說到葡萄酒，你有沒有注意到最近的梅洛特選紅酒有多棒？

Speaking of n.p., + clause.

講到……，……。

例 Speaking of cheese, have you tried this?

講到乳酪，你有試過這個嗎？

Speaking of Kate, I saw her in a bar last night with a weird foreigner!

講到凱特，我昨天在酒吧看到她和一個奇怪的老外在一起！

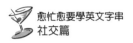
MP3 39

7 結束對話
Breaking off the conversation

Could you excuse me (for) a moment?
容我告辭一下好嗎？

Good/Nice talking to you.
很高興能夠和你聊天。

I have to be off.
我得走了。

I have to make a phone call.
我得打個電話。

I must just go and say hello to someone.
我得去跟別人打個招呼。

I need another drink.
我要再喝一杯。

I need to get some fresh air.
我需要一些新鮮空氣。

I want a cigarette.
我想要抽支菸。

I'll be back in a sec/second/minute/flash.

我很快就回來。

I'll be right back.

我馬上回來。

I'll catch you later.

待會兒見。

I'm just going to the bar/buffet.

我要去一下吧台／自助餐區。

If you'll excuse me a moment.

請容我告辭一下。

It's been nice talking to you.

很高興能和你聊天。

It's getting late.

現在有點晚了。

There's someone I want/need to talk to.

我想要／需要跟某個人談談。

Would you excuse me (for) a moment?

請你容我告辭一下好嗎？

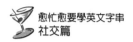
MP3 40

8 提議幫忙拿飲料
Offering to get a drink

Drink?
要喝的嗎？

Refill?[1]
要續杯嗎？

Can I get you a drink of something?
要我幫你拿什麼喝的嗎？

Can I get you something to drink?
要我幫你拿些喝的東西嗎？

Would you like a drink of something?
你想要喝點什麼嗎？

Would you like a drink?
你想要喝的嗎？

Can I get you a drink?
我能幫你拿杯飲料嗎？

Word list
① refill [rì`fɪl] *n.* 續杯

Would you like something to drink?

你想要喝點東西嗎？

Would anyone like another drink?

還有誰想要再來杯飲料嗎？

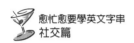
MP3 41

9 要求來一杯飲料
Asking for a drink

I'd like a nice stiff[1] drink.

我想要來一杯烈酒。

I need a drink.

我需要來一杯。

Can you get me a/another drink?

可以請你幫我拿／再拿一杯飲料嗎？

Could you get me something while you're up?

你可以順便幫我拿點東西嗎？

I'll take the same thing you're getting.

我要和你一樣的東西。

I could go for a n.p.

我可以來個……。

例 I could go for a Whiskey Sour.

我可以來一杯威士忌酸酒。

I could go for a shot of tequila.

我可以來一杯龍舌蘭。

Word list
① stiff [stɪf] *adj.* 烈的

222 →

對話範例

Brad: Hi. You enjoying the party?

Alice: Yes, actually. I don't really know anyone, but it's a nice place. Are you having a good time?

Brad: Yes. The drinks are very good! <u>I'm Brad, by the way</u>.

Alice: <u>Hello Brad. I'm Alice</u>. So what do you do?

Brad: <u>I'm in</u> finance. You?

Alice: Really? Me too. <u>I work for</u> an accountancy company called T&D. Maybe you've heard of them.

Brad: T&D? Oh yeah, sure. How long have you worked there?

Alice: About two years. And you? Are you based here?

Brad: No. Actually, <u>I'm based in</u> Shanghai. I'm just here for the conference. So, <u>I've heard</u> T&D is ....

布萊德：嗨，你還喜歡這場宴會嗎？

愛莉絲：嗯，很喜歡。我一個人都不認識，可是這個地方真不錯。你玩得開心嗎？

布萊德：是啊，酒很好喝！對了，我叫做布萊德。

愛莉絲：哈囉，布萊德，我是愛莉絲。你是做哪一行的？

布萊德：金融業。你呢？

愛莉絲：真的嗎？我也是。我在 T&D 會計事務所服務，也許你有聽過。

布萊德：T&D？喔，當然有。你在那裡服務多久了？

愛莉絲：兩年左右。你呢？你是在這裡工作嗎？

布萊德：不是，其實我是在上海工作，我只是來這裡開會而已。所以，我聽說 T&D……？

Mary: Have we met?

Mike: I don't think so. Mike.

Mary: Hello Mike. <u>My name's Mary</u>. <u>Pleased to meet you</u>.

Mike: <u>Pleased to meet you too</u>, Mary. So, what do you do?

Mary: <u>I work in</u> marketing. I'm a regional marketing manager for an IT company. Normally <u>I work out of Beijing</u>, but I'm here on business. My friend Kate over there, the one in the black sweater, she lives here and she invited me to this party. And you? How about you?

Mike: I live here. I was invited by Colin—he's the tall guy over there. He looks a bit drunk, actually.

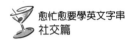
中譯

瑪莉：我們見過嗎？

麥克：我想沒有。我叫麥克。

瑪莉：哈囉，麥克。我叫瑪莉，很高興認識你。

麥克：我也是，瑪莉。妳是做哪一行的？

瑪莉：我是做行銷的。我是一家 IT 公司的地區行銷經理。我通常在北京工作，來這裡是為了公事。我朋友凱特在那邊，穿黑色毛衣那個，她住在這裡，所以就邀我來參加這場宴會。你呢？你怎麼會來這裡？

麥克：我住在這裡，是柯林邀請我來的，就是那邊那個高個子。他看起來真的有點醉了⋯⋯

3

Brad: ... so it's a potentially difficult situation.

Kate: Hello everyone.

Brad: Well, hi Kate.

Kate: Aren't you going to introduce me, Brad?

Brad: Oh, of course. <u>Kate, I'd like you to meet</u> Alice. Kate <u>has her own</u> fashion design company here in town, and Alice <u>works for</u> T&D.

Kate: T&D, huh? Nice work. <u>It's a pleasure</u>, Alice.

Alice: <u>Pleased to meet you too</u>, Kate.

Brad: We were just discussing the new business regulations, and Alice reckons they're going to impact small businesses worst.

Kate: I never talk about business after ten o'clock, Brad, as you know. *(laughter)* Now what I came over here to ask you was...

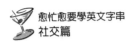
中譯

布萊德：……所以這可能會是個麻煩的情況。

凱　特：哈囉，各位。

布萊德：哦，嗨，凱特。

凱　特：你不介紹我嗎，布萊德？

布萊德：喔，當然要。愛莉絲，來見見凱特。凱特在市區開了一家時裝設計公司，愛莉絲則是在 T&D 服務。

凱　特：T&D 嗎？好工作。很高興認識你，愛莉絲。

愛莉絲：我也是，凱特。

布萊德：我們剛才在討論新的事業規定，而愛莉絲認為它們對小企業的影響最大。

凱　特：我從來不在十點過後談生意的。（笑）布萊德，你知道的。我來這是要問你……

Mike: ... well, I agree. Look. Here's Ms. Wong. Let's ask her about it. Hi Ms. Wong.

Ms. Wang: Hello.

Mike: Ms. Wong, <u>have you met</u> Mary? <u>Mary, meet Ms. Wong</u>. Ms. Wong <u>has her own IT company</u>, and Mary here is normally <u>based in</u> Beijing but is enjoying this fabulous party!

Mary: Hello Ms. Wong. <u>I'm Mary</u>.

Ms. Wang: Hi Mary. <u>Nice to meet you</u>.

Mike: We were just talking about Kate and how she knows so many people.

Ms. Wang: Oh yeah. She knows just about everybody. She's a great networker.

Mary: So how did you meet her, Ms. Wong?

Ms. Wang: Well, I used to date her brother. Then her brother married someone else and ...

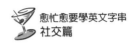

麥　克：……哦，我同意。你看，王小姐來了，我們來問問他。嗨，王小姐。

王小姐：哈囉。

麥　克：王小姐，你見過瑪莉嗎？瑪莉，來見見王小姐。王小姐開了一家 IT 公司，而瑪莉通常是在北京工作，但她現在正在享受這個很棒的宴會！

瑪　莉：哈囉，王小姐，我是瑪莉。

王小姐：嗨，瑪莉，很高興認識妳。

麥　克：我們剛才在談凱特，以及她怎麼會認識這麼多人。

王小姐：哦，對啊，她幾乎每個人都認識。她的人際關係真好。

瑪　莉：所以你是怎麼認識她的，王小姐？

王小姐：哦，我和她弟弟交往過，後來她弟弟跟別人結婚了……

George: Is there any more vodka in that bottle?

Sandra: Umm, I think there's enough for one more, yes.

George: Marvelous. Pass it over. <u>My name's George, by the way</u>.

Sandra: <u>Nice to meet you</u>, George. <u>I'm</u> Sandra.

George: So Sandra, what do you do?

Sandra: <u>I'm in</u> computing. <u>I work for</u> Yoyodyne.

George: Yoyodyne, eh?

Sandra: What do you do?

George: <u>I have my own</u> company that designs computer systems.

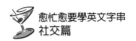

喬　　治：那個酒瓶裡還有沒有伏特加？

珊德拉：嗯，有，我想一個人喝應該綽綽有餘。

喬　　治：太好了，把它拿過來吧。對了，我叫喬治。

珊德拉：很高興認識你，喬治。我是珊德拉。

喬　　治：珊德拉，你是做哪一行的？

珊德拉：我是電腦業的，我在友友戴恩服務。

喬　　治：友友戴恩，是嗎？

珊德拉：你是做哪一行的？

喬　　治：我自己開公司設計電腦程式。

Mr. Wang: ... and finally the lawyers. So it's all very complicated.

Kate: Sounds terrible. Oh look. Here comes Mary.

Mary: Hello.

Kate: Mary, <u>have you met</u> Mr. Wang?

Mary: No, not yet.

Kate: Mr. Wang, <u>I want you to meet</u> Mary. Mary <u>is in</u> marketing, and Mr. Wang <u>runs his own</u> import-export company.

Mary: <u>It's a pleasure</u>, Mr. Wang.

Mr. Wang: <u>Pleased to meet you too</u>, Mary.

Kate: We were just talking about George. I think he's had too much to drink. He's been having a hard time recently, and he's been hitting the vodka rather hard.

中譯

王先生：……最後是律師。所以它真的很複雜。

凱　特：聽起來真麻煩。嘿，你看，瑪莉來了。

瑪　莉：哈囉。

凱　特：瑪莉，妳見過王先生嗎？

瑪　莉：沒有，還沒見過。

凱　特：王先生，我跟你引見一下瑪莉。瑪莉是做行銷的，王先生則是自己開進出口公司。

瑪　莉：很高興認識你，王先生。

王先生：我也是，瑪莉。

凱　特：我們剛才在聊喬治。我想他喝得太多了。他最近過得不太好，所以他喝了一大堆伏特加。

7

George: Who's that man over there talking to Brad?

Kate: Where? Oh, that's Mr. Wang.

George: He's very handsome, isn't he? What's he like?

Kate: He's very nice, actually, but rather eccentric.

George: Really? I love eccentric people.

Kate: Yes, but he may be too eccentric—even for you.

George: Why? What do you mean by that?

Kate: Well, haven't you heard?

George: Heard what? No one ever tells me anything.

Kate: <u>Well, apparently</u>, he's been having an affair with his secretary.

George: Really! How fascinating.

Kate: <u>According to</u> Mary, he's divorcing his wife and there's a big fight going on about the children. <u>I thought everyone knew</u>.

George: Well, what can I say—I didn't know. <u>Oh, I meant to tell you earlier</u>, your blouse doesn't really match your skirt. Those colors don't really suit you either.

Kate: Oh. Thanks. Look, <u>I must go and say hello to someone</u>. <u>I'll be right back</u>.

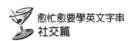

中譯

喬治：在那邊跟布萊德講話的男士是誰？

凱特：在哪？噢，那是王先生。

喬治：他真帥，對吧？他為人怎麼樣？

凱特：說真的，他人很好，可是很古怪。

喬治：是嗎，我喜歡古怪的人。

凱特：是啊，可是連妳都可能會覺得他太古怪了。

喬治：為什麼？妳這話是什麼意思？

凱特：哦，妳沒有聽說過嗎？

喬治：聽說什麼？從來沒人跟我說過什麼。

凱特：哦，他似乎跟他的秘書傳出了緋聞。

喬治：哇塞！太精彩了。

凱特：瑪莉說他正在和太太鬧離婚，而且為了小孩的事吵得很兇。我以為大家都知道。

喬治：哦，說真的，我不知道。對了，我剛才就想告訴妳，妳的衣服跟妳的裙子不太配。這些顏色也不太適合妳。

凱特：哦，謝謝。對了，我得去跟別人打個招呼，等下就回來。

Mike: Who's that tall guy over there?

Sandra: Oh. That's George. He looks very drunk.

Mike: What's he like normally?

Sandra: Normally, he's really reserved. But, <u>from what I hear</u>, he's got lots of problems.

Mike: Really? What kind of problems?

Sandra: Well, <u>off the record,</u> of course, I hear that he's got terrible debts. He has his own company, and it's not going very well.

Mike: Really? Well, I hate to say this, but I'm not surprised.

Sandra: Really? What makes you say that?

Mike: Well... he doesn't look very honest.

Sandra: I know—that's the problem. He can't find any customers. It's a pity, really, because his products are very good. <u>Oh. That reminds me</u>. Did I tell you about my new laptop?

Mike: Please, don't talk to me about laptops. Mine crashed on Friday and I lost everything. I hate them.

Sandra: Oh. Really?

Mike: Look, <u>I need another drink</u>. Do you want one?

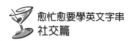
Sandra: Yes, please. I'll have another cocktail.

Mike:　　Vodka martini?

Sandra: Absolutely.

Mike　　I'll be back in a sec.

Sandra: OK. I'll wait for you here.

中譯

麥　克：那邊那個高個子是誰？

珊德拉：哦，那是喬治。他看起來醉得很厲害。

麥　克：他平常為人怎麼樣？

珊德拉：哦，他平常很含蓄。可是據我所知，他似乎有很多問題。

麥　克：是嗎？什麼樣的問題？

珊德拉：哦，別告訴別人，我聽說他負債累累。他自己開公司，但經營得不太好。

麥　克：真的嗎？我很不想這麼說，不過我並不意外。

珊德拉：是嗎，妳為什麼會這麼說？

麥　克：呃……他似乎不太老實。

珊德拉：我知道，問題就出在這裡。他根本找不到客戶。這真的很可惜，因為他的產品很好。對了，我突然想到，我有沒有跟你提過我的新筆記型電腦？

麥　克：拜託，別跟我提到筆記型電腦。我的電腦星期五掛了，資料全都不見。我氣死了。

珊德拉：哦，是嗎？

麥　克：對了，我要再喝一杯。你要嗎？

珊德拉：好，我還要一杯雞尾酒。

麥　克：伏特加馬丁尼是嗎？

珊德拉：沒錯。

麥　克：我等下就回來。

珊德拉：好，我在這裡等你。

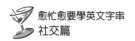

⑨

Mr. Wang: Who's that striking woman over there?

Kate: Hmm? Oh. That's Alice. She's totally mad. Don't get yourself in a room alone with her.

Mr. Wang: Really? Why not? She looks great.

Kate: Yes, I know, but she's dangerous.

Mr. Wang: Really? Tell me more.

Kate: Well, <u>I'm not one to gossip</u>, as you know, but rumor has it that she sued her former boss for sexual harassment.

Mr. Wang: You're kidding! So what happened?

Kate: Well, <u>this is just between us,</u> of course, but he was her lover and he wanted to leave her, so she got revenge—big time. I'll spare you the details, but let's just say she's a dangerous woman.

Mr. Wang: Wow.

Kate: <u>Oh, while we're on the subject</u>, what happened between you and your secretary?

Mr. Wang: What? I have no idea what you're talking about.

Kate: Oh, come on. Everybody knows.

Mr. Wang: <u>Could you excuse me for a moment</u>?

<u>I have to make a phone call</u>. *(exits)*

Kate:　　Oh, sure.

中譯

王先生：那邊那個大美女是誰？

凱　特：嘎？哦，那是愛莉絲。她根本是個瘋子，千萬不要跟
　　　　她獨處一室。

王先生：是嗎，為什麼？她看起來很不錯啊。

凱　特：是啊，我知道，可是她很危險。

王先生：是嗎，再說多一點。

凱　特：哦，你也知道我不愛說長道短，不過有傳聞說，她告
　　　　她的前任老闆性騷擾。

王先生：真的嗎？結果呢？

凱　特：這個嘛，千萬不要說出去，他們兩個是一對，而他想
　　　　要離開她，於是她就報復他。我聽他說，她是個危險
　　　　的女人。

王先生：哇。

凱　特：對了，既然我們聊到了這件事，你跟你的秘書怎麼樣
　　　　了？

王先生：我不知道你在說什麼。

凱　特：你得了吧，大家都知道。

王先生：容我告辭一下好嗎？我得打個電話。（離開）

凱　特：哦，當然好。

Part 6
談論電影

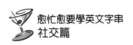
MP3 43

1 正面評論
Positive

I'm crazy about n.p.

我很瘋⋯⋯。

例 I'm crazy about gangster movies.

我很瘋幫派電影。

I'm crazy about Japanese cartoons. They're so cute!

我很瘋日本卡通。它們實在太可愛了!

I love n.p.

我很愛⋯⋯。

例 I love documentaries.

我很愛看記錄片。

I love westerns. I like cowboys!

我很愛看西部片。我喜歡牛仔!

I really like n.p.

我真的很喜歡⋯⋯。

例 I really like long epics.

我真的很喜歡史詩鉅片。

I really like musicals. They make me feel good.

我真的很喜歡歌舞片。它們讓我覺得很開心。

N.p. is really good.

……真的很棒。

例 That movie is really good.

那部電影真的很棒。

The Godfather is really good. If you haven't seen it, you should.

《教父》真的很棒。如果你還沒看過，你應該要看一看。

I quite like n.p., especially when + clause.

我相當喜歡……，特別是……的時候。

例 I quite like horror movies, especially when I watch them with my girlfriend.

我相當喜歡恐怖片，特別是和我女友一起看的時候。

I quite like road movies, especially when they are set in America.

我相當喜歡馬路電影，特別是以美國為場景的時候。

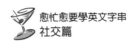
I'm rather keen[1] on n.p.

我相當熱衷於……。

例 I'm rather keen on kung fu movies.

我相當熱衷於功夫電影。

I'm rather keen on war movies.

我相當熱衷於戰爭電影。

N.p. is OK.

……還算可以。

例 *Batman* is OK. It's not fantastic, but it's OK.

《蝙蝠俠》還算可以。它不是很精彩,但還算可以。

Saving Private Ryan is OK, but it's not Tom
Sizemore's best movie.

《拯救雷恩大兵》還算可以,但它不是湯姆‧西斯摩爾最好的
片子。

Word list

① keen [kin] *adj.* 熱衷的;沉迷的

2 負面評論
Negative

I can't stand n.p.

我很受不了……。

例 I can't stand horror movies. I hate being scared.

我很受不了恐怖電影。我痛恨被嚇到。

I can't stand gangster movies. I don't like the violence.

我很受不了幫派電影。我不喜歡暴力。

I can't bear n.p.

我無法忍受……。

例 I can't bear cartoons. I find them pointless and stupid.

我無法忍受卡通。我覺得它們既無意義又愚蠢。

I can't bear war movies. I think they are obscene.[1]

我無法忍受戰爭電影。我覺得它們很討厭。

I really don't like n.p.

我真的很不喜歡……。

Word list

① obscene [əb`sin] *adj.* 令人厭惡的

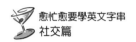

例 I really don't like cartoons. I think they are taste-less rubbish.

我真的很不喜歡卡通。我覺得它們是毫無品味的垃圾。

I really don't like westerns. Cowboys bore me.

我真的很不喜歡西部片。牛仔讓我覺得很無聊。

I don't really like n.p.

我不是很喜歡……。

例 I don't really like *The Godfather* movies. They are too long!

我不是很喜歡《教父》系列的電影。它們實在有夠長！

I don't really like art house movies. I find them a bit slow and boring.

我不是很喜歡藝術電影。我覺得它們步調有點慢又無聊。

I'm not so keen on n.p.

我不太熱衷……。

例 I'm not so keen on road movies. I don't like traveling myself, so watching other people do it is awful.

我不太熱衷馬路電影。我本身就不喜歡旅行，所以看別人旅行更糟。

I'm not so keen on sequels and prequels. Once is enough!

我不太熱衷續集和前傳。看一次就夠了！

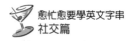
MP3 45

3 電影和影片類型
Movie and film genres

action film 動作片

animated movie 動畫電影

cartoon 卡通

art (house) movie 藝術（工作室）電影

biopic [ˈbaɪopɪk] 傳記片

blue movie / porn 情色電影／色情片

cable movie 有線電影

comedy 喜劇片

costume drama 古裝劇情片

crime film 犯罪片

documentary 記錄片

epic 史詩片

fantasy 奇幻片

film noir [ˈfɪlm ˈnwɑr] 黑白片

gangster movie 幫派電影

horror movie 恐怖電影

kung fu movie 功夫電影

musical 歌舞片

prequel [`prikwl̩] 前傳

road movie 公路電影

romantic comedy 浪漫喜劇

science fiction 科幻片

sequel [`sikwəl] 續集

spy movie 間諜電影

straight-to-video movie 直接發行錄影帶的電影

straight-to-DVD movie 直接發行 DVD 的電影

B movie B 級片

supernatural thriller [ˌsupəˋnætʃərəl ˋθrɪlə]
超自然驚悚片

thriller 驚悚片

war movie 戰爭電影

western 西部片

I saw a good/bad n.p. last night
我昨晚看了一部很棒／很爛的……。

例 I saw a good romantic comedy last night.
  我昨晚看了一部很不錯的浪漫喜劇片。

  I saw a bad cartoon last night.
  我昨晚看了一部很爛的卡通

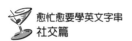

I really like/dislike n.p.

我眞的很喜歡／不喜歡……。

例 I really like westerns.

我真的很喜歡西部片。

I really dislike documentaries.

我真的很不喜歡記錄片。

4 電影卡司和工作人員
Cast and crew

art director 藝術指導

assistant director 副導演

camera man/camera operator 攝影師／掌鏡者

cast 卡司

casting director 選角指導

composer 配樂製作者

director 導演

director of photography/cinematographer
[ˌsɪnəmə`tɑɡrəfə] 攝影指導／攝影者

distributor 出品者

editor 剪接

executive producer 監製

female lead 女主角

male lead 男主角

production designer 美術設計

property manager 道具管理

screenwriter 編劇

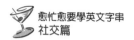
sound director 音效指導

foley artist 音效剪接

stand in/double 替身

star 明星

stuntman [ˋstʌntˏmæn] 特技演員

supporting role 配角

The n.p. is/was X

⋯⋯是⋯⋯。

例 The male lead was Chow Yun-Fat.

男主角是周潤發。

The supporting role is played by Brad Pitt.

配角是布萊德彼特。

5 談論電影的 Chunks
Chunks for talking about movies

adapt a screenplay 改編劇本

例 They adapted the screenplay from a novel.

他們將小說改編成劇本。

be ahead of schedule 進度超前

例 Apparently, filming on the new Spiderman movie is ahead of schedule! The producers are very pleased.

顯然新《蜘蛛人》電影的拍攝進度超前！製片們都非常高興。

be behind schedule 進度落後

例 Because they had to fire the star and hire a new one to take over, filming is behind schedule.

由於他們必須開除那個明星並雇用新人來接手，所以拍攝進度落後了。

be on schedule 按照進度

例 It's on schedule. Everything is going according to plan.

進度準確。一切都按照計畫進行中。

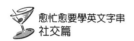
be over budget   超出預算

例 There were delays because of bad weather. Since this caused some unexpected costs, they are over budget.

氣候不佳而造成了延宕。由於產生了一些事前沒有預料到的成本，他們超出了預算。

be within budget   預算之內

例 So far there are no problems, and everything is within budget.

目前為止沒有發生任何問題，一切都在預算之內。

go on general release   全面上映

例 It goes on general release next month in the States, and then the month after that, it goes on general release globally.

它下星期在美國全面上映，然後再下個月會在全球全面上映。

play a character   飾演一角

例 He plays three different characters in the same movie! He's amazing!

他在同一部電影裡飾演三個不同的角色！他真是太厲害了！

play a part　飾演一角

例 Brad plays that part really well. It's such a good part for him.

布萊德把那個角色演得非常好。那個角色很適合他。

shoot some footage[1]　拍一些畫面

例 The director and cinematographer shot some footage together before they started filming the movie to show prospective[2] investors how the film would look.

導演和攝影師在拍片前一起拍了些畫面，讓可能的投資者看看片子會是什麼樣子。

take a shot　拍攝

例 They had to take that shot twenty-seven times because the actors couldn't stop laughing.

他們必須拍攝那個鏡頭二十七次，因為演員不停笑場。

write a screenplay　寫劇本

例 The screenwriter wrote the screenplay when he was a student.

編劇在他學生時期就寫好了劇本。

Word list

① footage [ˈfʊtɪdʒ] *n.* （影片的）呎數；長度
② prospective [prəˈspɛktɪv] *adj.* 未來的；預期的

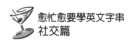
be in 有演

例 Julia Roberts is in it.
茱莉亞‧羅伯茲有演這部片。

be out 推出

例 It will be out next month.
它下個月會推出。

be on at 在……上映

例 I think it's on at the Breeze Center.
我想它有在微風廣場上映。

It's on at 9:00 on channel 7.
它是九點在第七台上映。

be by 執導

例 It's by Steven Spielberg.
它是由史蒂芬‧史匹柏執導。

be about 是關於

例 It's about this guy who wants to have a sex change.
它是關於一個想要變性的男子。

be from　來自

例 It's from Hollywood, of course, but it was filmed in Canada. I hear production costs are cheaper there.

它是來自好萊塢,但在加拿大拍攝的。我聽說那裡的製作成本比較低。

be made in　拍攝於

例 It was made in Prague, which looks like old Paris.

它是拍攝於布拉格,那裡看起來像以前的巴黎。

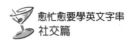 對話範例

Kate: Have you seen the new Wobert D. Nearo movie?

Brad: Is that the animated one?

Kate: Yeah, it's really good.

Brad: I don't really like cartoons.

Kate: Really? I love them! They're so cute!

Brad: I find them boring. I prefer gangster movies.

Kate: Oh yeah? I really don't like gangster movies. I don't like on screen violence. What's your favorite movie?

Brad: I think *The Business Godfather* is the best one. You?

Kate: Part one or part two?

Brad: Actually part two is better.

Kate: Yes, I agree. Part three is terrible. Randy Gracias is in it, right?

Brad: Yes, that's right, and it was made in Rome. It's not so good. You know it took ages to make, and was behind schedule and over budget.

Kate: Really?

Brad: Yeah. And they had problems with the <u>cast</u>. Most of them didn't like the star, and the <u>male and female leads</u> had an off-screen romance. The <u>female lead</u> got pregnant, which made <u>shooting the movie</u> difficult. I also heard that the <u>director</u> and <u>executive producer</u> kept fighting.

Kate: Wow. It must be so difficult to make a movie, actually, if you think about it: so many people to manage, and so many things to organize.

Brad: Yes. My company is <u>financing a movie</u> at the moment.

Kate: Really?

Brad: Yes, a low budget <u>art house movie</u>, but our CEO believes in supporting the arts.

Kate: Oh, so do I.

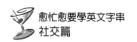

凱　特：你看了瓦勃迪尼洛的新電影嗎？

布萊德：是那部動畫片嗎？

凱　特：是啊，那部片很好看。

布萊德：我不太喜歡看卡通。

凱　特：是嗎？我愛死了！它們實在好可愛！

布萊德：我覺得它們很無聊。我寧可去看幫派電影。

凱　特：是哦？我不太喜歡幫派電影，因為我不喜歡銀幕暴力。你最喜歡什麼電影？

布萊德：我覺得最棒的是《The Business Godfather》。你呢？

凱　特：第一集還是第二集？

布萊德：說實話，第二集比較好。

凱　特：沒錯，我同意。第三部就很差了，藍迪格瑞西亞斯有演，對吧？

布萊德：對，沒錯，而且它是在羅馬拍攝，只是拍得不怎麼樣。你知道它拍了好久，進度落後又超出預算。

凱　特：是嗎？

布萊德：是啊，而且他們的卡司也有問題。他們大部分的人都不喜歡那個明星，而且男女主角又鬧出戲外緋聞。結果女主角懷孕了，而這也提高了電影拍攝的難度。我還聽說，導演和攝影師從頭吵到尾。

凱　特：哇，說真的，拍電影一定很難。你想想看，有這麼多人要打點，又有這麼多事要安排。

布萊德：是啊。我公司目前就在出資拍電影。

凱　特：真的嗎？

布萊德：真的，是一部低預算的藝術電影，可是我們老闆認為
　　　　要支持藝術。

凱　特：喔，我有同感。

Socializing

Part 7
談論音樂

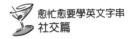 **MP3 49**

1 關於音樂的詞彙
Musical terms

album 專輯

例 It's one of my favorite albums.

這是我最喜歡的專輯之一。

alto [ˈælto] 女低音

例 She's got this beautiful low alto voice which sounds like chocolate!

她的聲音是美妙的女低音，聽起來就像巧克力一樣！

backing vocals 合音

例 The backing vocals were better than the main singer!

合音比主唱歌手還要好！

band 樂團

例 The band was excellent. We asked them to play an encore.

這個樂團非常厲害。我們要求他們演奏安可曲。

baritone [ˈbærəˌton]　男中音

例 My favorite baritone is Herman Prey.

我最喜歡的男中音是赫爾曼‧普雷。

bass　男低音

例 I sing bass in my local church choir.

我在我社區教堂唱詩班裡唱男低音。

brass instruments [ˈbræs ˈɪnstrəmənt]　銅管樂器

例 My son wants to learn to play a brass instrument, but he can't decide which one.

我兒子想要學習演奏一種銅管樂器，但是他沒辦法決定要學哪一種。

chamber music　室內樂

例 I prefer chamber music to large symphony[1] orchestras.[2]

我喜歡室內樂勝過大型交響樂管弦樂團。

choral [ˈkɔrəl] **music**　合唱音樂

例 I like Spanish choral music. We sing a lot of it at church.

我喜歡西班牙合唱音樂。我們在教堂常常唱。

Word list

① symphony [ˈsɪmfənɪ] *n.* 交響樂
② orchestra [ˈɔrkɪstrə] *n.* 管弦樂團

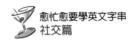

composer 作曲家

例 My favorite composer is Mozart.

我最喜歡的作曲家是莫札特。

concert 音樂會

例 I went to this excellent concert last night at the National Concert Hall.

我昨晚去聽一場在國家音樂廳的超棒音樂會。

concerto [kən`tʃɛrto] 協奏曲

例 His first piano concerto is my favorite piece of classical music.

他的第一首鋼琴協奏曲是我最喜歡的古典樂作品。

conductor 指揮家

例 There are very few female conductors in the world. It seems to be a man's job.

世上的女性指揮家很少。這似乎是個男性的工作。

duet [du`ɛt] 二重奏

例 She plays violin and I play piano, so we sometimes get together and play as a duet.

她拉小提琴、我彈鋼琴,所以我們有時候會聚在一起演奏二重奏。

gospel choir [`gɑspḷ`kwaɪr] 福音合唱團

例 I love gospel choirs—they are so inspiring!

我很喜歡福音合唱團，它們真是太發人省思了！

hit single 熱門單曲

例 His latest hit single was incredible!

他最新的熱門單曲好聽極了！

jingle 廣告歌

例 The jingle on that commercial really irritates me. I can't get it out of my head!

那個廣告的廣告歌實在有夠討厭，一直在我腦中揮之不去！

keyboard instrument 鍵盤樂器

例 My daughter is studying piano. She can play synthesizer[1] and organ.[2]

我的女兒在學鋼琴。她會彈電子琴和風琴。

lead singer 主唱

例 The lead singer looks like a woman but is actually a guy.

那個主唱看起來像是個女的，但其實他是男的。

Word list

① synthesizer [`sɪnθə͵saɪzə] *n.* 電子琴

② organ [`ɔrgən] *n.* 風琴

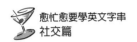
live recording　現場錄音

例 It's a live recording so the sound quality is not so good, but the playing is awesome.

這是現場錄音，所以音質沒有那麼好，但是演奏部分真是出神入化。

opera　歌劇

例 *The Phantom of the Opera* is not a true opera. It's really a musical.

《歌劇魅影》不是真正的歌劇，它其實是齣音樂劇。

opera diva　歌劇首席女角

例 Maria Callas was the greatest opera diva of all time.

瑪麗亞‧卡拉絲是有史以來最棒的歌劇女伶。

pop group　流行樂團

例 I used to play in a pop group in high school. We sounded terrible, but we sure did have fun!

我以前中學時參加過一個流行樂團。我們彈得很遜，但是我們玩得很開心！

quartet [kwɔrˋtɛt]　四重奏

例 He used to play with the Miles Davis jazz quartet.

他以前和邁爾斯戴維斯爵士四重奏一起演奏。

quintet [kwɪn`tɛt]　五重奏

例 Schubert wrote some beautiful quintets.
舒伯特寫了一些很優美的五重奏。

record company　唱片公司

例 The record companies are really suffering from
the increase in piracy.[1]
唱片公司都飽受盜版氾濫之苦。

record label　唱片公司

例 That record label only specializes in jazz
recordings.
那個唱片公司只專攻爵士樂。

rock star　搖滾巨星

例 Elvis Presley was a great rock star.
貓王是一個偉大的搖滾巨星。

sonata [sə`nɑtə]　奏鳴曲

例 I like Schubert's last piano sonatas best. They
are very moving.
我最喜歡舒伯特的最後幾首鋼琴奏鳴曲。它們非常能夠感動人
心。

Word list
① piracy [`paɪrəsɪ] *n.* 盜版；侵害著作權

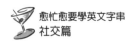

song writer 作（詞）曲者

例 She's a song writer as well as singer, did you know?

她既是詞曲創作者也是歌手，你知道嗎？

soprano [sə`præno] 女高音

例 The soprano sang so high!

那個女高音唱得好高！

string instrument 弦樂器

例 String instruments are very difficult to learn to play.

弦樂器很難學會演奏。

symphony [`sɪmfənɪ] 交響曲

例 Did you know that Beethoven, Schubert, and Mahler all died after completing their ninth symphonies?

你知道貝多芬、舒伯特和馬勒都是在完成第九號交響曲後過世的嗎？

tenor [`tɛnə] 男高音

例 When I was young I was a tenor, but now I'm a baritone.

我年輕的時候是個男高音，但是現在成了男中音。

trio [ˈtrio] 三重奏

例 There's nothing better than a good jazz trio!
沒有什麼比好的爵士三重奏更棒的了！

wind instrument 管樂器

例 He can play any kind of wind instrument—it's amazing!
他會吹奏任何種類的管樂器，真是太驚人了！

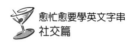
MP3 50

2 談論音樂帶來的感受
Talking about the effects of music

快樂的 Happy

cheerful 開心的

triumphant [traɪ`ʌmfənt] 意氣風發的

ecstatic [ɛk`stætɪk] 狂喜的

lighthearted [`laɪt`hɑrtɪd] 輕快的

playful 俏皮的

悲傷的 Sad

nostalgic [nɑs`tældʒɪk] 懷舊的

full of longing 渴望的

introspective [ˌɪntrə`spɛktɪv] 自省的

heartbroken 心碎的

gloomy 憂傷的

活力充沛的 Energetic

funky 放克（一種節奏感強的音樂類型）風格的

thrilling 刺激的

exhilarating [ɪgˋzɪləˏretɪŋ]　快活的

wild　狂放的

uplifting [ʌpˋlɪftɪŋ]　振奮的

放鬆的　Relaxing

calming　穩定心神的

soothing　舒緩的

lulling [ˋlʌlɪŋ]　安撫的

consoling　撫慰的

peaceful　平和的

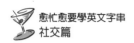
MP3 51

3 概略地談論音樂
Being vague about music

... sort of ...
……有點……

例 Those trumpets[1] sound sort of triumphant.

那些小號聽起來有點意氣風發的感覺。

The bases playing that low, slow tune sound sort of gloomy.

貝斯演奏如此低沉、緩慢的曲調聽起來有點憂傷。

... kind of ...
……有些……

例 That fast rhythm sounds kind of exhilarating, don't you think?

那些輕快節奏聽起來有些快活，你不覺得嗎？

Those high notes sound kind of lighthearted, kind of happy, you know?

那些高音聽起來還滿輕快、也滿快樂的，你懂嗎？

Word list
① trumpet [ˋtrʌmpɪt] *n.* 小喇叭；小號

... or anything ...

……或其他什麼的……

例 It sounds like it hasn't got a tune or anything.

它聽起來根本沒有旋律或其他什麼的。

There's no melody or anything—it's just noise to me.

這根本沒有旋律或其他什麼的——在我聽來只是噪音。

... like ...

……像是……

例 It's just a lot of banging, like someone falling down stairs!

這只是一堆敲擊聲，像是有人摔下樓梯！

It sounds calming, like a green meadow, you know?

這聽起來滿能穩定心神的，像是一片綠野，你懂嗎？

... or something ...

……之類的……

例 It's like jazz or something, but it was written two hundred years ago!

這很像爵士之類的，但是它兩百年前就寫出來了！

It sounds like a storm at sea or something.

它聽起來像是一場海上風暴之類的。

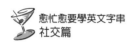
It's hard to describe, but + clause.

它很難形容，不過……。

例 It's hard to describe, but I find it very uplifting. It makes me think of God.

它很難形容，不過我覺得它能振奮人心，讓我想到上帝。

It's hard to describe, but I find this kind of music quite consoling.

它很難形容，不過我覺得這種音樂滿能撫慰人心的。

It's difficult to say, but + clause.

我說不太上來，但是……。

例 It's difficult to say, but the cello has a kind of introspective sound.

我說不太上來，但是大提琴好像有一種發人深省的聲音。

It's difficult to say, but the tune sounds so full of longing. I don't know what it's longing for!

我說不太上來，但是這個曲調聽起來是如此地充滿了渴望。我不知道它渴望的是什麼！

It's not easy to put into words, but + clause.

這很難用言語形容，但是……。

例 It's not easy to put into words, but it's very funky, it makes me want to dance!

這很難用言語形容，但是它放克風格強烈，讓我想要跳舞！

It's not easy to put into words, but it sounds so playful with all those fast little notes!

這很難用言語形容，但是它那些輕快的小聲音聽起來好俏皮！

I can't really describe it, but + clause.

我沒辦法形容，但是……。

例 I can't really describe it, but it's like singing someone to sleep.

我沒辦法形容，但是這就像在唱歌哄人睡覺。

I can't really describe it, but it's a very exhilarating tune!

我沒辦法形容，但是這是個非常令人快活的曲調！

I'm not sure how to put it, but + clause.

我不曉得要怎麼說，但是……。

例 I'm not sure how to put it, but it sounds like a heartbroken person crying.

我不曉得要怎麼說，但是它聽起來像是一個心碎人的哀泣。

I'm not sure how to put it, but it's quite nostalgic, like the music my grandparents listened to when they were young and in love.

我不曉得要怎麼說，但是它像是在懷念往日時光，就像是我祖父母年輕時陷入愛河會聽的音樂。

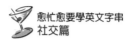
... —do you know what I mean?

……──你知道我是什麼意思嗎?

例 It's like the voice of God—do you know what I mean?

這像是上帝之聲──你知道我是什麼意思嗎?

It sounds really ecstatic and happy—do you know what I mean?

這聽起來非常地狂喜歡樂──你知道我是什麼意思嗎?

對話範例

Sandra: Hi, Colin. What's that you're listening to?

Colin: Hmm? Oh, this? It's Miles Davis. His last <u>album</u>.

Sandra: Oh. You like jazz, do you?

Colin: Oh, yeah. In a big way. You?

Sandra: Well, I like some kinds of jazz. I like big <u>band</u> music, for example. But <u>classical music</u>'s more my thing. I like going to <u>chamber music concerts</u>.

Colin: Me, too. But I like going to listen to jazz trumpet.

Sandra: Really? Do you play?

Colin: Yes, a bit—unfortunately for my neighbors! You?

Sandra: I played the violin when I was a kid, but I stopped when I left school.

Colin: Oh, listen to this.

Sandra: Wow, it's really <u>exciting</u>!

Colin: Isn't it? Just listen to that bass.

Sandra: Yeah. I like it. <u>It's hard to describe, but it's kind of ... uplifting</u>?

Part 7 談論音樂

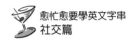
Colin: It's <u>funky</u>, man! Funky!

 中譯

珊德拉：嗨，柯林。你在聽的是什麼音樂？

柯　林：嗯？這個嗎？這是邁爾斯・戴維斯的上一張專輯。

珊德拉：哦。你挺喜歡爵士樂的，對吧？

柯　林：對啊，可以說相當喜歡。妳呢？

珊德拉：嗯，有幾種爵士樂我還滿喜歡的，像我就滿喜歡大樂
　　　　團音樂。不過，我更喜歡古典樂。我喜歡聽室內音樂
　　　　會。

柯　林：喔，我也是。不過我喜歡聽的是爵士喇叭。

珊德拉：喔，是嗎？你會吹嗎？

柯　林：會一點，不過鄰居就倒楣了。妳呢？

珊德拉：我小時候會拉小提琴，不過畢業以後就沒再拉了。

柯　林：我了解。喔，天哪，妳聽聽這個。

珊德拉：哇，真令人興奮！

柯　林：不是嗎。聽聽裡面的低音。

珊德拉：喔，聽到了，我喜歡。它很難形容，不過讓我覺得很
　　　　……振奮？

柯　林：那是放克音樂，嘿！放克！

🍷 Part 8

談論書籍

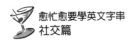
1 正面評論
Positive

fully drawn characters　有深度的角色

gripping[1] plot　引人入勝的情節

important message　重要的訊息

plausible[2] events　寫實的事件

vivid description　生動的描述

witty dialogue　詼諧的對話

Word list
① gripping〔ˋɡrɪpɪŋ〕 *adj.* 引人入勝的
② plausible〔ˋplɔzəb!〕 *adj.* 似真實的；寫實的

2 負面評論
Negative

flat description　平淡的描述

implausible events　難以信服的事件

predictable events　沒有創意的事件

trivial[1] message　不重要的訊息

one-dimensional[2] characters　沒有深度的角色

wooden dialogue　呆板的對話

Word list
① trivial [ˈtrɪvɪəl] *adj.* 不重要的；瑣碎的
② one-dimensional [ˈwʌn.dəˈmɛnʃənl] *adj.* 沒有深度的

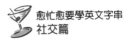
MP3 55

3 談論書籍
Talking about a book

What's that you're reading?
你在看的那本是什麼書？

Reading anything right now?
現在有在看什麼書嗎？

Have you read any good books lately?
你最近有看過什麼好書嗎？

What's it about?
它是關於什麼的？

Tell me about it.
跟我分享一下吧。

What happens in the book?
書中的故事是什麼？

Is it any good?
它好看嗎？

I'm reading something by X.

我正在看……的作品。

例 I'm reading something by Thomas Pynchon.

我正在看湯瑪斯·品瓊的作品。

I'm reading something by a French author.

我正在看一個法國作家的作品。

I'm reading this ... about ....

我在看這本……，它是關於……。

例 I'm reading this detective story about a guy looking for his wife's killer.

我在看這本偵探小說，它是關於一個想找出殺妻兇手的人。

I'm reading this fantasy novel about a ring that controls man's fate.

我在看這本奇幻小說，它是關於一個控制人類命運的戒指。

It's the latest ... by X.

這是……最新的……。

例 It's the latest best seller by Quentin Brand.

這是昆廷·布蘭德的最新暢銷作品。

It's the latest thriller by Dan Brown.

這是丹布朗最新的驚悚小說。

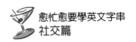

It's really adj., full of n.p.

它非常地……，裡面充滿了……。

例 It's really well written, full of interesting characters.

它寫得非常好，裡面充滿了有趣的角色。

It's really boring, full of unrealistic dialog.

它非常地無聊，裡面充滿了不真實的對話。

It's ... about ....

它是……，講的是……。

例 It's a travel book about a guy who travels across Asia.

它是一本旅遊書，講的是一個遊遍亞洲的旅人。

It's a science fiction novel about a computer hacker who steals information.

它是一本科幻小說，講的是一個偷取資料的電腦駭客。

... bring sth. out ...

……出版……

例 Beta is bringing out several new books in the fall.

貝塔將在秋天出版一些新書。

Sth. comes out ....

……出版。

例 His new book is coming out in the fall.

他的新書將在秋天出版。

... get sth. across ...

……傳達……

例 Her new book really gets her message across.

她的新書充分傳達了她的訊息。

Sth. comes across ....

……被理解。

例 Her message really comes across in her new book.

她的訊息在她的新書中被充分理解。

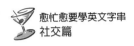

 書籍種類
The types of books

a play 劇本

authorized biography 授權的傳記（非主角親自撰寫，而是寫者經由主角或其家人的協助而寫成）

unauthorized biography 未授權的傳記（非主角親自撰寫，也未經由主角或其家人的協助）

autobiography 傳記

classic novel 古典小說

criticism 評論

detective story 偵探故事

ghost story 鬼故事

history 歷史

horror story 恐怖故事

modern classic 現代經典

novella [no`vɛlə] 中篇小說

philosophy 哲學

poetry anthology [ˋpɔɪtrɪ ænˋθɑləd3ɪ] 詩文選集

pulp fiction 通俗小說

self development manual/self help manual
勵志書

short story 短篇故事

thriller 驚悚小說

travel book 旅遊書

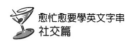
 MP3 57

 對話範例

Brad: <u>What's that you're reading</u>?

Kate: This? Oh, <u>it's the latest novel by Pam Wheeler</u>.

Brad: Oh, right. Any good?

Kate: Yes, it's not bad. It's got a <u>gripping plot</u>, and <u>the dialog is quite witty</u>.

Brad: <u>What's it about</u>?

Kate: <u>It's about sex and shopping</u>, really. The superficiality[1] of the 1980s really <u>comes across</u>.

Brad: Yes, I read her first book.

Kate: Oh, yes, that's a classic of its kind. Did you like it?

Brad: It was certainly a page-turner.[2]

Kate: So <u>what are you reading</u>?

Brad: <u>I'm reading this travel book about a train journey across Mongolia</u>.

Kate: Wow, sounds good.

Brad: Yes, <u>it's really interesting, full of wonderfully vivid descriptions of landscapes</u>. The only trouble is it's taking me ages to read.

Kate: Why's that?

Brad: Well, it's a really heavy book, and the binding[3] is broken, so I can't carry it around with me. I can only read it at home.

Word list
① superficiality [ˌsupɚˌfɪʃɪˈæləti] *n.* 膚淺
② page-turner [ˈpedʒˌtɜnɚ] *n.* 讓人手不釋卷的書
③ binding [ˈbaɪndɪŋ] *n.* 裝訂

中譯

布萊德：妳在看的那本是什麼書？

凱　特：這本嗎？哦，這是帕恩惠勒最新的小說。

布萊德：原來如此。好看嗎？

凱　特：嗯，還不錯。它的情節不賴，對白也寫得很好。

布萊德：它在講什麼？

凱　特：它其實是在談性別與購物。它很能反映出 1980 年代
　　　　的膚淺。

布萊德：的確，我看過她的第一本書。

凱　特：喔，對啊，它可說是同類的經典之作。你喜歡嗎？

布萊德：它絕對是一本引人入勝的書。

凱　特：那你在看什麼？

布萊德：我在看這本旅遊書，它講的是橫跨蒙古的火車之旅。

凱　特：哇，聽起來不錯。

布萊德：是啊，有趣得很，裡面充滿了對景色極為生動的描
　　　　述。唯一的麻煩是，我得花很長的時間來讀完。

凱　特：哦，為什麼會這樣？

布萊德：這本書好重，而且裝訂的地方又散了，所以我沒辦法
　　　　隨身攜帶。我只有在家時才能讀它。

Part 9
談論運動

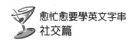

1 談論運動
Talking about sports and exercise

MP3 58

It makes me feel really adj. when + clause.

當……的時候，我覺得非常……。

例 It makes me feel really healthy when I'm working out.

當我在健身的時候，我覺得非常健康。

It makes me feel really cool when I'm all dressed up in my workout gear![1]

當我全身穿著健身服時，我會覺得非常酷。

Afterwards I feel so adj.

事後我覺得好……。

例 Afterwards I feel so relaxed.

事後我覺得好放鬆。

Afterwards I feel so exhausted.

事後我覺得精疲力竭。

Word list
① gear [gɪr] *n.*（供某種用途之）服裝

While I'm doing it, I feel so adj.

當我在做的時候，我覺得好……。

例 While I'm doing it, I feel so stupid. I think everyone must be watching me.

當我在做的時候，我覺得好蠢。我想大家一定都在看我。

While I'm doing it, I feel so focused and clear.

當我在做的時候，我覺得既專注又清醒。

It does me good.

這對我有好處。

例 It's a fast rough game. It does me good. It keeps
me fit.

它是節奏快又累人的運動。這對我有好處，可以讓我維持身
材。

It's slow and relaxing. It does me good. Helps me
to unwind¹ after a hard day.

它的節奏慢又放鬆。這對我有好處，幫助我在辛苦的一天後舒
緩下來。

Word list

① unwind [ʌn`waɪnd] *v.* 使身心放鬆

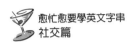
I really get a kick out of it.

我非常樂在其中。

例 I go three times a week. I really get a kick out of it.

我一週去三次，我非常樂在其中。

I don't do it as often as I would like. I really get a kick out of it, so I guess I should do it more often, right?

我想要常做，但未能如願。我非常樂在其中，所以我想我應該更常做，對吧？

It helps (me) to V.

它有助（我）……。

例 It helps me to relax after a hard day.

它有助我在辛苦的一天後放輕鬆。

It helps to reduce my cholesterol.[1]

它有助於降低我的膽固醇。

Word list
① cholesterol [kə`lɛstə,rol] *n.* 膽固醇

2 從事某項運動的說法
Verbs for doing sports

以下的運動，在前頭加上動詞 play。

soccer 足球

football 橄欖球

basketball 籃球

volleyball 排球

golf 高爾夫球

tennis 網球

ping-pong 乒乓球

rugby [ˈrʌgbɪ] 英式橄欖球

以下的運動，在前頭加上動詞 do。

a workout 健身

exercise 運動

athletics 體育運動

aerobics [ˌeəˈrobɪks] 有氧運動

yoga 瑜珈

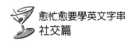
tai chi　太極

martial [ˈmɑrʃəl] **arts**　功夫

以下的運動，在前頭加上動詞 go。

climbing　爬山

jogging　慢跑

swimming　游泳

running　跑步

hiking　健行

sailing　航海

diving　潛水

skiing　滑雪

3 談論高爾夫球
Talking about golf

on the range 在練習場上

例 When I'm on the range practicing my stroke, I feel really happy!

當我在練習場上練習揮桿時，我覺得非常開心！

on the course 在高爾夫球場上

例 It's quite windy out on the course today.

今天高爾夫球場上的風很大。

play a shot 揮桿

例 He played such a great shot on the last hole.

他在上一洞揮出絕妙的一桿。

select a club 選擇球桿

例 Steve Webster says the key to winning is selecting the best club for the conditions.

史蒂夫・韋伯斯特說過，贏球的關鍵在於視情況選出最適合的球桿。

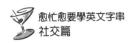
line of putt 推桿線；球的行進路線

例 My line of putt was wrong, so I didn't get the ball in the hole.

我的路徑不對，所以我沒有把球打進洞裡。

early holes 前幾洞

例 I'm quite good at the early holes, but then later in the game I start to get nervous and I usually mess up.

我在前幾洞都表現不錯，但之後在比賽裡我就開始緊張，常常搞砸。

finishing holes 最後幾洞

例 Of course the finishing holes are the most difficult.

當然最後幾洞是最難的。

practice tee[1] 球座；球墊

例 I got this great practice tee and it really helped me to improve my stroke.

我有一個很棒的球座，它著實讓我的揮桿更進步了。

Word list
① tee [ti] *n.* 球座

smooth backswing 順暢的向後拉桿

例 My coach says the key is having a smooth backswing.
我的教練說，關鍵在於順暢的向後拉桿。

shoot into the 70s 打出低於 70 桿的成績

例 After a couple of lessons, I was able to shoot into the 70s with not much effort.
在上過幾堂課後，我可以不費力地打出低於 70 桿的成績。

on the green 在果嶺上

例 His strength as a player is on the green.
他身為球手，最大的強項是在果嶺上。

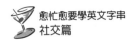

MP3 61

4 談論網球
Talking about tennis

tied thirty-thirty　二比二平手

例 They tied thirty-thirty in the third set. It was such an exciting moment!

他們在第三盤以二比二平手。那真是刺激的一刻！

match point　決勝點（決定贏球或輸球的那一分）

例 They reached match point after one hour and thirty minutes. It was such a fast game.

他們在一個半小時後到達決勝點。這場比賽進行得真快。

game, set, and match　比賽結束（贏得比賽時，裁判會說的話）

例 You win, game, set, and match! Congratulations!

你贏了，比賽結束！恭喜！

be up in the second set　在第二盤領先

例 He started badly but he was up in the second set. I didn't see how it ended, but I think he won.

他一開始打得不好，但是在第二盤領先。我沒有看到結尾，但是我想他贏了。

go to the semi-finals/finals 進入準決賽／決賽

例 She won that match so she goes to the semi-finals for the first time in her career.

她贏了那一場，所以她進入了職業生涯中的第一場準決賽。

clip[1] the net 觸網

例 He lost the point because the ball just clipped the net.

他因為球觸網而失去那一分。

superb volley[1] 高超的截擊（指球還沒落地就把它打回去）

例 It was a superb volley. The crowd went nuts!

那是一記高超的截擊，群眾都欣喜若狂！

lose his/her serve 輸掉發球局

例 When she gets nervous, she loses her serve.

她一緊張起來，就會輸掉發球局。

Word list
① clip [klɪp] *v.* 打中
② volley [ˋvɑlɪ] *n.* 截擊

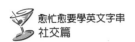
change sides　換邊

例 Halfway through the game they change sides to make it fair.

比賽進行到一半，他們換邊以保持公平。

rain stopped play　雨中斷了比賽

例 It was just getting really exciting when rain stopped play. We all had to take cover and wait for the storm to pass.

比賽正在刺激的時刻，雨卻中斷了比賽。我們都得去躲雨，等待暴雨過去。

a formidable[1] backhand[2]　讓人難以招架的反手拍

例 He's got the most formidable backhand of anyone in the game.

在參賽者中，他的反手拍無人能及。

be seeded first / second / third / fourth, etc.

排名第一／第二／第三／第四（以此類推）的種子球員

Word list

① formidable [ˈfɔrmɪdəbl] *adj.* 難以對付的；令人畏懼的

② backhand [ˈbæk`hænd] *n.* 反手拍

例 She's so young but she's already seeded fourth in the world. What a talent!

她這麼年輕，但卻已經是全球排名第四的種子球員。真是個天才！

ace 發球得分

例 He scored thirty-one aces in one game! Incredible, just incredible!

他一場比賽裡總共三十一次發球得分！真厲害，實在太厲害了！

教父小叮嚀

● 網球的分數是從 love（0 分）算起，然後 15、30、40 分，最後則是 game。假如兩個球員都拿到 40 分，就稱為 deuce，而接下來的那分則叫做 advantage。此時必須超前兩分，才能贏得該局。

● Set「盤」最少是由六個 games「局」所組成。先贏得六局的人就算贏得該盤。若對方已經贏了五局，此時你必須贏他兩局來阻止他獲勝，並要增加局數來決定勝負。Match 所包含的 set 從二到五個不等。

MP3 62

5 談論足球
Talking about soccer

a penalty kick　罰球

例 They won the game on a penalty kick.

他們靠著一記罰球贏得這場比賽。

penalty area　禁區

例 He should have stayed out of the penalty area while the goalkeeper[1] had the ball.

他原本應該在守門員拿到球時留在禁區外的。

injury time　傷停時間（裁判延長比賽的時間，以彌補球員受傷所耗損的時間）

例 They added forty minutes to the game for injury time.

他們把比賽延長了四十分鐘作為傷停時間。

foul[2] sb.　對某人犯規

例 He was sent off the field because he fouled the other side's captain.

他因為對對方隊長犯規而被驅逐出場。

Word list
① goalkeeper [ˋgol͵kipɚ] *n.* 守門員
② foul [faʊl] *v.* 犯規

an equalizer[1]　追平的同分球（指球隊進球，使雙方的分數相同）

例 They only won because they scored an equalizer.
他們之所以會贏，純粹是因為他們踢進一球追平分數。

full time　比賽時間結束

例 At full time the score was still nil-nil.
比賽結束時，雙方比數仍然零比零。

decided on penalties　以罰球定勝負

例 That match was decided on penalties. It wasn't a very exciting game.
那場比賽是以罰球定勝負，不是非常精彩的比賽。

end in a draw　平手

例 As always, when these two teams play each other, it ended in a draw.
一如往常，這兩隊對戰結果是平手。

Word list
① equalizer [`ikwəl͵aɪzə] *n.* 同分球

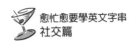

lead one-nil / lead one-nothing　一比零領先

（nil 是英式英語；lead one-nothing 為美式說法）

例 Currently Manchester United are leading one-nil.
I think they're going to win.

目前曼聯以一比零領先。我想他們會贏。

yellow card　黃牌

例 The referee handed out four yellow cards! The
crowd and teams were furious.

裁判遞出四張黃牌！群眾和球隊都氣炸了。

 教父小叮嚀

● 在錦標賽中，假如比賽到正規時間結束還是不分勝負，兩隊要各罰
踢五球來決定誰勝誰負。

● 當球員粗暴地對別人作出犯規動作或故意犯規時，裁判就會對他舉
yellow card。假如球員在同一場比賽出現兩次這種情形，他就會被
舉紅牌並驅逐出場。

6 談論健身
Talking about working out

work out 健身

例 I always work out in the morning because the gym is quieter and less crowed then.

我總是在早上健身，因為那時健身房比較安靜，人也比較少。

burn off 消耗

例 I want to burn off some of those calories I ate last night.

我想要消耗一些我昨晚吃進去的卡路里。

work off 紓解

例 I'm under a lot of stress at work and the gym is a good place to work it off.

我工作的壓力很大，而健身房是個紓解壓力的好地方。

warm up 熱身

例 Because she forgot to warm up before her exercise class, she injured her back.

她因為忘記在上運動課前先熱身，才會弄傷了背。

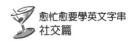
cool down 做緩和運動

例 It's important to cool down after strenuous¹ exercise.

在激烈運動後，很重要的一件事就是要做緩和運動。

give up 放棄

例 Even when I feel exhausted after twenty minutes of jogging, I never give up. I always try to run for thirty (minutes).

就算我在慢跑二十分鐘後精疲力竭，也從來不會放棄。我總是試著跑三十分鐘。

stick to it 持之以恆

例 Find a form of exercise that you like and then stick to it.

找一種你喜歡的運動，然後持之以恆。

be into 喜歡

例 I'm really into my gym instructor, he's so cool!

我真的很喜歡我的健身房教練，他很酷！

Word list
① strenuous [ˋstrɛnjuəs] *adj.* 激烈的

work up a (good) sweat 運動到流（滿身）汗

例 You only really lose weight if you work up a good
sweat when exercising.

你若真的要減肥，唯一的辦法就是運動到流滿身汗。

add more weights 多加一些重量

例 I thought I was doing really well, and then the
instructor added more weights to the exercise
machine.

我覺得我原先做得還不錯，結果教練竟然又在運動器材上多加
了些重量。

get (back) into shape 練好身體

例 It's so difficult to get back into shape after I don't
exercise for a while.

在我停止運動一陣子後，要再把身體練好真是困難啊。

follow a routine 做固定的一套運動

例 If you follow a routine, it's easier to make sure
you get a balanced workout.

如果你做固定的一套運動，就比較容易確保自己有均衡的運
動。

Part
9
談
論
運
動

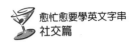
number of reps　重覆的次數（每項運動所做的次數）

例 I found my workout really difficult, so my instructor reduced the number of reps.

我發現我的健身訓練太困難，所以我的教練把次數給減少了。

maintain motivation　保持動力

例 To maintain motivation, I look in the mirror and imagine how slim I want to be!

為了保持動力，我看著鏡子，想像自己要變得多苗條！

對話範例

Sandra: You play golf, don't you?

Colin: Yep. Twenty years—and on golf courses all over the world.

Sandra: Well, my handicap is fourteen, but I still dream of <u>shooting into the 70s</u> someday. My boss is disgusted with the way I play. Any tips?

Colin: Actually, it's all a question of mindset. What do you think your strengths are?

Sandra: Well I'm pretty good <u>on the range</u> and the <u>practice tee</u>, but when I get <u>on the course</u>, it all goes to pieces.

Colin: Well that's a pretty common problem. Are your <u>early holes</u> better than your <u>finishing holes</u>?

Sandra: Hmm, yes, actually they are.

Colin: Well, my advice is this: when you're <u>on the greens</u>, choose the <u>line of putt</u> carefully and stroke the ball. When you're <u>playing a shot</u>,

Part
9

談
論
運
動

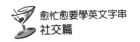
<u>select your club</u> carefully, and try to get a
<u>smooth backswing</u>.

Sandra: Well, thanks! Can I get you a drink?

珊德拉：你打高爾夫球吧，是不是？

柯　林：是啊！20 年了，世界各地的球場都去過了。

珊德拉：嗯，我的差點是 14，但我還是夢想有一天能有 70
　　　　桿以下的成績。我老闆很厭惡我的打球方式，有任何
　　　　訣竅嗎？

柯　林：呃，這全是心態的問題。你認為你有什麼優勢？

珊德拉：嗯，我在練習場打得很好，開球也不錯，但開始比賽
　　　　時，這些都消失殆盡了。

柯　林：嗯，這是個很常見的問題。你前幾洞的成績是不是比
　　　　後幾洞的成績好？

珊德拉：呃……，沒錯，正是如此。

柯　林：嗯，我的建議是這樣的：當你在果嶺時，謹慎挑選一
　　　　個路徑，然後擊球。輪到你打球時，謹慎挑選球桿，
　　　　做好向後的拉桿動作。

珊德拉：喔，謝了。我可以請你喝杯飲料嗎？

Brad: What's the score?

Kate: Fisher is up five games to four, but it's <u>tied thirty-thirty</u> now. Martina <u>was up in the first set</u> but she <u>lost her serve</u>. Then <u>rain stopped play</u>, and when they came back and <u>changed sides</u>, she never recovered.

Brad: Hmm. English weather—typical. Wow, that was a <u>superb volley</u>.

Kate: I know. Fisher's got the most <u>formidable backhand</u>. Ohh! Fisher <u>clipped the net</u> but it still went over!

Brad: Oh, dear. Fisher has pulled ahead. Who do you want to win?

Kate: Well, if Martina wins she'll <u>go to the semi-finals</u>, but Fisher <u>is seeded fourth</u>, so it's going to be hard for her. Oh my goodness! It's <u>match point</u> already! Hush.

...

Kate: <u>Ace! Game, set, and match</u>! She's won! Fantastic!

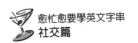

布萊德：現在比數多少？

凱　特：Fisher 和 Martina 各勝五和四局，現在比數是二比
二。 Martina 在第一盤原本領先，但她輸掉了擁有
發球權的那一局。後來雨中斷了比賽，當她們再度回
到場上，換邊比賽後，她就每況愈下。

布萊德：嗯，真是典型的英國氣候，哇！那真是一個精彩的截
擊。

凱　特：沒錯，Fisher 的反手拍無人能比。哦！ Fisher 觸
網，但球還是過了。

布萊德：哦！ Fisher 領先了。你希望誰贏？

凱　特：嗯，如果 Martina 贏了，她就可以進入準決賽，不
過 Fisher 是排名第四的種子選手，所以對她而言並
不是件易事。喔，天啊！已經是決定勝負關鍵的一分
了，安靜！

……

凱　特：發球得分！比賽終了！她贏了，真是太棒了！

③

Alice: What's the score?

George: United is <u>leading one-nil</u>.

Alice: Crap!

George: The other side has <u>a penalty kick</u> now because Becky <u>fouled someone</u> inside the <u>penalty area</u>.

Alice: Oh.

George: It's tense, man. The referee's been handing out <u>yellow cards</u> all over the place.

Alice: Yeah, but don't worry. If it's one-nil, United will hold on to win.

George: Right, but I want the other side to win! Take the ball!! Take the ball!! Ooooooh! He's such a lousy player!

Alice: I think the best you can hope for is <u>an equalizer</u> during <u>injury time</u>.

George: If the other team scores, I reckon it will <u>end in a draw</u> at <u>full time</u>. It's too bad, only tournament matches are <u>decided on penalties</u>.

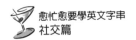

愛莉絲：比數是多少？

喬　治：United 以一比零領先。

愛莉絲：哎呀！

喬　治：由於 Becky 在禁區內犯規，對方得到一個罰球的機會。

愛莉絲：哦！

喬　治：天呀！真緊張！裁判到處舉黃牌！

愛莉絲：是呀，但不用擔心，如果比數是一比零，United 會繼續領先。

喬　治：是呀！但我希望另一方會贏。搶球！搶球！呃！他真是個差勁的球員。

愛莉絲：我想你最多只能期望在傷停時間時能來個同分。

喬　治：如果對方得分，我認為在比賽終了時雙方比數會相同。太可惜了，只有錦標賽會以二隊各罰踢五球來決定勝負。

(4)

Sandra: Hi, Brad. I haven't seen you here before!

Brad: Hey, Sandra. Oh, yeah? I come here regularly every other morning.

Sandra: Oh, right. I usually come in the evening, but I just joined a few weeks ago. I'm trying to <u>get into shape</u> for the summer.

Brad: Oh, good. Are you <u>following a routine</u>?

Sandra: Yes, I'm doing abs and thighs, some work on the mats, and then I do half an hour of jogging to <u>work up a good sweat</u>. What about you? You look pretty buff.

Brad: Oh, really? Thanks. Well, I'm just doing my normal workout. I'm trying to increase the <u>number of reps</u> I'm doing on this machine, as I want to strengthen my lower back. I've <u>added some more weights</u>, so it's kind of hard at the moment because I'm not used to it. I also need to <u>burn off</u> some of last night's beer, so I'm going to run a couple of miles on the treadmill.

Sandra: Wow, you sound really <u>into it</u>. It's really good for <u>working off</u> stress, isn't it, coming here?

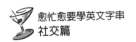

Brad: Well, sometimes it's hard to <u>maintain motivation</u>, especially if you're really busy, but it's important to find a routine that works for you and <u>stick to it</u>.

Sandra: Yeah, don't give in, right. No pain; no gain.

Brad: You got it. Also, don't forget to <u>warm up</u> properly otherwise you'll hurt yourself, and <u>cool down</u> afterwards, as well.

Sandra: That's good advice. Well, catch you later.

Brad: You too, man. Enjoy your workout.

Sandra: Same to you.

珊德拉：嗨，布萊德，我以前沒在這裡看過你！

布萊德：嗨，珊德拉。是嗎？我每隔一個早上都會固定來這裡。

珊德拉：難怪，我通常是晚上來，不過我是前幾個星期才加入的。我想在夏天來臨前練好身體。

布萊德：喔，不錯。你有固定做什麼運動嗎？

珊德拉：有，我會練腹肌和大腿，在墊子上做一些伸展運動，然後慢跑半小時，讓身體痛快地流汗。你呢？你看起來體格很棒。

布萊德：哦，真的嗎？謝謝。我只有做普通的運動而已。我試著增加在這台機器上鍛鍊的反覆次數，因為我想要強化我的下背部。我多加了一些重量，我還沒習慣，所以目前有點費力。我還要把昨晚喝的一些啤酒消耗掉，所以我打算在跑步機上跑個幾哩。

珊德拉：哇，聽起來你真是投入。來這裡紓解壓力是很棒的事，對吧？

布萊德：嗯，保持動力有時候還挺難的，尤其是很忙的時候。但重點在於，要找一套對自己有用的固定運動，然後持之以恆。

珊德拉：沒錯，不要放棄。沒有耕耘就不會有收穫。

布萊德：你說得對。此外，不要忘了適度地熱身，否則你就會受傷，而且事後還要做緩和運動。

珊德拉：這個建議不錯。好了，待會兒見。

布萊德：你也是，老哥。好好練喔！

珊德拉：你也是。

Part
9
談論運動

Part 10
道別

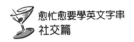
MP3 65

1 示意要離開
Signaling to leave

說話者 A—陳述（Statement）

Well, I have to be making a move soon.
好了，我馬上就得走了。

I really must be going.
我真的得走了。

I'd best be on my way.
我最好上路了。

Gosh, look at the time.
老天，看看都什麼時候了。

Gosh, is that the time?
天啊！那是現在的時間嗎？

I'd better be off.
我最好趕快走了。

It's time to go.
該走了。

It's high time I left.
是我該離開的時候了。

Got to go.
得走了。

說話者 B—回應（Response）

So soon? Are you sure?
這麼快？你確定嗎？

Oh, that's a pity. Can't you stay a bit longer?
喔，真可惜。你不能再留一會兒嗎？

Stay for one more drink.
再留下來多喝一杯吧！

Have another one before you go.
再喝一杯再走吧。

Yes, I suppose I'd better be off, too.
嗯，我想我最好也趕快走了。

OK. Let's pay the tab/bill.
好，我們來付帳吧。

Yeah, it's past my bedtime, too.
嗯，也過了我的睡覺時間了。

All right. Want to split a cab?
好。想要搭同一部計程車嗎？

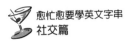
MP3 66

2 致謝
Thanking

說話者 A—陳述（Statement）

Thank you for a lovely evening.

謝謝你給了我這個美好的夜晚。

It was a wonderful evening.

這是個美好的夜晚。

Thanks for breakfast/lunch/dinner.

謝謝你招待的早餐／午餐／晚餐。

Thanks for the coffee/drink.

謝謝你招待的咖啡／飲料。

It's been good meeting you.

很高興和你見面。

I've enjoyed working with you.

我很高興和你一起工作。

You've been very helpful.

你幫了很大的忙。

I hope to see you again next year.

我希望明年可以再見到你。

It's been nice to meet you.
很高興能見到你。

說話者 B─回應（Response）

No, thank you!
不，應該是我要謝謝你！

The pleasure was mine.
我才應該感到榮幸。

It's been a pleasure having you.
很高興有你加入。

It's been good meeting you.
很高興和你見面。

My pleasure.
我的榮幸。

Not at all.
不客氣。

You're very welcome.
你不用客氣。

We should do it again sometime.
我們應該找時間再來聚聚。

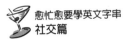
Let's do it again soon.
我們要儘早再聚聚。

3 離開
Leaving

See you soon.
不久後見。

See you again soon.
稍後再見。

See you later.
稍後見。

Talk to you soon.
稍後再聊。

Bye.
拜。

Bye-bye.
拜拜。

Good-bye.
再見。

See you.
再見。

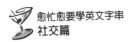
說話者 B—回應（Response）

Have a safe trip.

路上小心。

Have a good journey.

祝你旅途愉快。

Give my regards to X.

替我向⋯⋯問好。

Give my best wishes to X.

代我向⋯⋯獻上誠摯問候。

Give X my best wishes.

代我向⋯⋯獻上誠摯問候。

Take care.

保重。

Keep in touch.

保持聯絡。

Don't be a stranger.

有空常聯絡。

對話範例

①

Brad: OK. <u>Got to go</u>.

Alice: <u>Yes, I suppose I'd better be off, too</u>.

Brad: <u>Thanks for lunch</u>.

Alice: <u>Not at all</u>. <u>Let's do it again soon</u>.

Brad: OK. <u>See you later</u>.

Alice: <u>See you</u>.

中譯

布萊德：好了，該走了！

愛莉絲：嗯，我最好也趕快離開了。

布萊德：謝謝你招待的午餐。

愛莉絲：不客氣，有空再一起用午餐。

布萊德：沒問題，再見！

愛莉絲：再見！

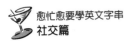

Mary: <u>Gosh, is that the time</u>?

Mike: Yes, it's late, isn't it?

Mary: Look, <u>I'd better be off</u>. I've got an early flight tomorrow.

Mike: Oh, no—<u>stay for one more drink</u>.

Mary: Thanks, but <u>I really must be going</u>. <u>Thank you for a lovely evening</u>.

Mike: Oh, <u>you're very welcome</u>. <u>It's been a pleasure having you</u>.

Mary: Right. <u>See you soon</u>.

Mike: Yes, <u>keep in touch</u>. <u>Give my regards to</u> Kate.

Mary: I will. <u>Bye</u>.

Mike: Bye.

中譯

瑪莉：天啊！時間是這樣嗎！

麥克：是啊，已經很晚了，不是嗎？

瑪莉：嗯，我得走了，我明天一早還有班機得趕！

麥克：哦，不，再留下來多喝一杯吧！

瑪莉：謝謝，但我真的得走了。謝謝你給了我這個美好的夜
晚。

麥克：不客氣，很高興和妳聚聚！

瑪莉：是呀，再見！

麥克：好，保持聯絡，替我向凱特問好。

瑪莉：我會的，再見。

麥克：再見。

專為華人商務人士完整歸納
愈忙愈要學英文系列

風行 500 大企業的 Leximodel 字串學習法,從此不必學文法!

想穩站職涯巔峰,必須掌握英文實力與專業能力的雙重優勢!
現在起,學會Leximodel字串學習法及chunks、set-phrases、word partnerships三大字串,
寫道地的英文Email、秀專業的英文簡報、說漂亮的社交英文、show英文提案,
職場表現當然No1!

愈忙愈要學
英文簡報

愈忙愈要學
英文提案與報告

愈忙愈要學
100個商業動詞

▼1書2CD
定價:380元

愈忙愈要學
社交英文

愈忙愈要學
英文Email

▲1書1CD
定價:350元

▲1書1MP3
定價:380元

▲1書1DVD
定價:280元

▲定價:280元

{商務菁英‧聯名推薦}

台灣先靈事業處資深經理　**李業寧**
證券暨期貨市場發展基金會總經理　**邱靖博**
上海商銀副總經理　**邱怡仁**
AIG友邦信用卡總經理　**卓文芬**

台灣電通公司資深營業總監　**鄭長銓**
安侯建業會計師事務所會計師　**林寶珠**
美商聯眾人力資源部經理　**陳玲玲**

國家圖書館出版品預行編目資料

愈忙愈要學英文字串——社交篇 = Biz English for
Busy People: Mini Book - Socializing / Quentin
Brand 作. ——初版.——臺北市：
貝塔，2007〔民96〕
　　面：　　　公分
ISBN 978-957-729-643-6（平裝附光碟片）

1. 英國語言 — 會話

805.188　　　　　　　　　　　　　　96004238

愈忙愈要學英文字串——社交篇
Biz English for Busy People: Mini Book—Socializing

作　　者 / Quentin Brand
譯　　者 / 何岱耘
執行編輯 / 陳家仁、官芝羽

出　　版 / 貝塔出版有限公司
地　　址 / 台北市 100 館前路 12 號 11 樓
電　　話 / (02)2314-2525
傳　　真 / (02)2312-3535
郵　　撥 / 19493777 貝塔出版有限公司
客服專線 / (02)2314-3535
客服信箱 / btservice@betamedia.com.tw

總 經 銷 / 凌域國際股份有限公司
地　　址 / 台北縣泰山鄉漢口街 38 號
電　　話 / (02)2908-1100
傳　　真 / (02)2908-1155

出版日期 / 2007 年 5 月初版一刷
定　　價 / 220 元
I S B N：978-957-729-643-6

Biz English for Busy People: Mini Book—Socializing
Copyright 2007 by Quentin Brand
Published by Beta Multimedia Publishing

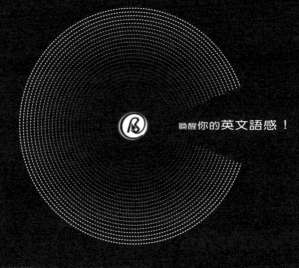

喚醒你的**英文語感**！

請對折後釘好，直接寄回即可！

| 廣　告　回　信 |
| 北區郵政管理局登記證 |
| 北台字第14256號 |
| 免　貼　郵　票 |

100 台北市中正區館前路12號11樓

 貝塔語言出版 收
Beta Multimedia Publishing

寄件者住址 ☐☐☐

謝謝您購買本書！！

貝塔語言擁有最優良之英文學習書籍，為提供您最佳的英語學習資訊，您可填妥此表後寄回（免貼郵票）將可不定期免費收到本公司最新發行書訊及活動訊息！

姓名：_____ 性別：□男 □女 生日：_____年_____月_____日

電話：(公)_____(宅)_____(手機)_____

電子信箱：_____

學歷：□高中職含以下 □專科 □大學 □研究所含以上

職業：□金融 □服務 □傳播 □製造 □資訊 □軍公教 □出版 □自由 □教育 □學生 □其他

職級：□企業負責人 □高階主管 □中階主管 □職員 □專業人士

1. 您購買的書籍是？_____

2. 您從何處得知本產品？(可複選)

　　□書店 □網路 □書展 □校園活動 □廣告信函 □他人推薦 □新聞報導 □其他

3. 您覺得本產品價格：

　　□偏高 □合理 □偏低

4. 請問目前您每週花了多少時間學英語？

　　□不到十分鐘 □十分鐘以上，但不到半小時 □半小時以上，但不到一小時

　　□一小時以上，但不到兩小時 □兩個小時以上 □不一定

5. 通常在選擇語言學習書時，哪些因素是您會考慮的？

　　□封面 □內容、實用性 □品牌 □媒體、朋友推薦 □價格 □其他_____

6. 市面上您最需要的語言書種類為？

　　□聽力 □閱讀 □文法 □口說 □寫作 □其他_____

7. 通常您會透過何種方式選購語言學習書籍？

　　□書店門市 □網路書店 □郵購 □直接找出版社 □學校或公司團購

　　□其他_____

8. 給我們的建議：_____

喚醒你的英文語感！

Get a Feel for English !

喚醒你的英文語感！

Get d